RED HOPE

BOOK 1

JOHN DREESE

Cover art by James at www.GoOnWrite.com

Edited by Kristen Warthen and Jason Defenbaugh.

Email: JJDreese@yahoo.com
Web: http://www.dreesecode.com/redhope/
Twitter: http://www.twitter.com/JJDreese/
Amazon Kindle Version available from:
      http://www.amazon.com/dp/B00RA7QOHY
Version 1.452p

Published in the United States of America.

For Lee, Daniel, Caroline,
George, and Martha

ACKNOWLEDGEMENTS

This book was written with the support of many helpful people. I am forever grateful to them.

My wife Lee supported this project in many ways, from read-throughs to moral support. Jason Defenbaugh was an editor from the very beginning when the book consisted of one chapter. Yulia Gaydutskaya helped make sure the Russian names were realistic. Kristin Warthen helped me find my missing commas, but ended up fixing my grammar as well as making the book easier to read. Elena Greer taught me the importance of character dialogue. Jan Batts is an author and journalist whose contagious enthusiasm inspired me to follow through on this story. Chris Sideroff shared some of his wit and funny stories. Pointwise helped me find President Daggett Jennings. Jason and Estee Valendy helped clarify part of the story that needed to be just right. Last, but not least, is Kurt Chankaya. His stories about the scientific exploration of Mars were my first real introduction to the idea of manned missions to the Red Planet.

Thank you, everybody. Enjoy.

PREFACE

"As I take man's last step from the surface, back home for some time to come – but we believe not too long into the future – I'd like to just [say] what I believe history will record. That America's challenge of today has forged man's destiny of tomorrow. And, as we leave the Moon at Taurus-Littrow, we leave as we came and, God willing, as we shall return: with peace and hope for all mankind. Godspeed the crew of Apollo 17."

The words shown above were spoken live from the Moon by Astronaut Gene Cernan. He said them as he left the last human boot print there on December 14, 1972. I was launched into existence the very next year, but by then the Apollo Lunar program had been officially mothballed. My generation has never known the excitement of watching people walk on another celestial body.

Instead, call us the *space shuttle generation*. In the second grade, my class watched the first shuttle launch on live television. These events were commonplace by the time my seventh grade teacher announced the explosion of the Challenger. Seventeen years later, I woke up to the grinding sound of the Columbia breaking up in the skies high above my apartment in Fort Worth, Texas.

Nearly three decades after watching that very first launch through a second-grader's eyes, I sat in my cubical at work and grimly watched, via the internet, the last shuttle lift off. America's manned access to space was over.

Here we are on the cusp of 2015 and hope springs eternal. The era of the space shuttle has come and gone. We now rely on Russia for access to space. However, in that great American spirit of stumbling our way to success, we have a few companies with great prospects ahead of them. These are the likes of Blue Origin, Orion, and Whittenberg Space Launch Systems.

They might not be replacements for the space shuttle, but they are major stepping stones to mankind's next giant leap: Mars. Hopefully, I'll get to watch people walking on the Red Planet someday. Where we go after that will be up to the next generation. Having missed out on the whole Mars quest, they'll be itching for an adventure of their own.

John Dreese

The Artifact

CHAPTER 1

The White House
Washington, D.C.

Good news is rarely born after midnight. A ringing telephone cracked open the silence just before 3:00 a.m. It rattled on an antique nightstand, only an arm's reach away from the most powerful leader of the free world.

Hours earlier, President Daggett Jennings had finished the first campaign fundraiser of what was sure to be a long season. Collapsing poll numbers forced the process on him much earlier than usual this time around. When tonight's event was over, the president staggered into bed, barely conscious — his head melted into the pillow.

The phone kept ringing, finally jolting the president out of his slumber. He reached out of bed to pick up the receiver and brought it back to his ear.

"Hello," he groaned.

"Sorry to wake you at this hour, Mr. President," the voice of the overnight operator apologized. "But the director of NASA is trying to reach you. He says it's *urgent*. Shall I patch him through?"

"Not again," the president complained.

"Excuse me, sir?"

"Oh, nothing," the president said. "Please patch him through. Thanks."

The NASA director was an old friend. The president had to take this call. After he heard the phone call transfer click, the president cleared his throat with a cough and asked, "Chris, are you bleeding to death? Because you better be to call me this late."

On the other end of the phone was the longtime head of NASA, a short man named Chris Tankovitch who sported a full head of dark black hair. He had a beet-red face and looked like the poster child for hypertension. Chris was taken aback by the irritation buried in the president's voice, but nothing was going to stop him tonight.

"I have some incredible news that can't wait until morning," Chris said with excitement. "It's going to change our lives *forever.*"

President Jennings let out a painful sigh. "Wait, wait, wait. Is this about the budget meeting tomorrow? Because that can wait. Really. *Good night,* Chris."

"No, wait, hang on!" Chris begged. "This is more of an *interplanetary* issue, okay? Look, I don't think the budget will be a problem after tonight."

That caught the president's attention.

"Okay, tell me what it is," the frustrated president demanded. He glanced over to see if the phone call woke up his wife. It did. She stared back with worry.

Miles away, Chris smiled in anticipation. "It's something that I have to show you in person."

The president imagined Chris pushing his glasses back

up onto his nose as he talked.

"All right, come on over. I'll tell the guards to expect you."

The president hung up the phone. He leaned over to give his wife a kiss on the forehead.

"I'll be back in a little bit," he whispered.

"Everything okay?" she asked with a groggy voice.

"Yes, it's just Chris. He's got another wild hair up his rear end that he needs to talk about."

"I hope that's figurative," she laughed. "Go easy on Chris. He's the only reason you passed physics."

The president chuckled. "I know, I know, and that's why I made him the director of NASA."

He sat up on the bed, put his feet on the floor, and his hands on his knees. His brain was still foggy from being in such a deep sleep.

The presidency had grayed his hair and drained the part of his soul which hadn't been auctioned off during his rise to power. He breathed slowly, desperately wanting to close his eyes and slip back into sleep. Still in his pajamas, he wandered haphazardly toward the door, quietly opened it, and disappeared down the darkened hallway.

Just outside the White House, the head of NASA ran up the sidewalk after going through the security gate. The cool night breeze tried to shake the papers out of his tightly gripped hands. It only managed to mess up his hair. His cellphone was alive with beeps and blinking lights. Messages were rolling in for him even at this early hour. His expression was a mix of determination and excitement.

Chris finally arrived at the main door. A Secret Service

agent let him in.

He stepped into the Oval Office where the president was already sitting and sipping a cup of coffee. Chris was amped up and knew he wouldn't sleep for days. The president stood up and shook Chris's hand in that political, two-fisted type of handshake.

"Chris, you look like death warmed over," the president chided.

"Well, it's been a long night," Chris complained.

The president pointed toward the sofa and said in a fatherly voice, "All right. Have a seat. Have a seat right there. Would you like some coffee?"

Chris declined with the wave of his hand. The president motioned for the night butler to leave the room.

As they both sat down, the president said, "Please tell me what all the fuss is about."

"I'll get right to it, DJ —"

"Stop right there," the president interrupted. "Please show some respect for this office. I worked hard to get here."

The awkward silence that followed was a bookend on nearly twenty-five years of friendship, one which started when they attended the Ohio State University together. That was now the past and no longer mattered. Chris understood.

"Okay. *Mr. President*," Chris said apologetically.

"See? That's more like it. Please continue."

"So, *Mr. President*, as you know, we sent a rover called Curiosity to Mars, right? Well, it's been driving around for years, digging holes and running tests with extremely advanced scientific equipment. It's found some evidence of ice below the surface and we've learned some amazing things about the geology of the red planet. With regards to life, however, it hasn't really found anything. Just traces of organic gases."

Chris's arms shot into the air to emphasize his frustration.

The president nodded and said, "Yes, of course. I remember when it landed. It was a proud moment for our country. That engineer with the mohawk and all."

"Yes, that's the one," Chris agreed with a head nod. "It really was a proud moment. We sent all of that scientific equipment to Mars, you know, to hopefully find signs of life, whether it be bacteria, or lichen or something. Anything, really. It would be the greatest discovery of our lifetime. But most importantly, it would justify my budget requests."

Chris laughed at his own comment.

The president shifted in his chair, obviously getting more interested in what the NASA director was itching to tell him. A similar meeting had taken place years before, but that discovery hadn't panned out. The president was still skeptical about what Chris was going to say, but admittedly he was curious.

"Mr. President," he said, quickly pausing for effect.

"Mr. President, we just found signs of life. Ironically, we didn't need any scientific equipment. All we needed was a camera," Chris said as his serious face opened up to a smile. His arms spread out wide to personify the word *WOW*.

The president sat upright.

"Well, what did you find?" the president asked, suddenly excited. "Plants? Animals? I thought Mars was too cold for life. Speak up man!"

"No sir, we found fossils."

The president's brow furrowed, "A fossil?"

"No, I said fossils."

The president rolled his eyes at the correction.

Chris realized his social blunder and quickly said, "Yes, but not the kind we'd hoped for or ever expected."

As Chris spoke so enthusiastically, he pulled out a photo marked "D" in the corner. He delicately turned it around to reveal a black and white image to the president. The word fossil was reverberating in both of their minds now.

The president took the photo and eased back into his chair to soak in the image. He took a deep breath; his left eyebrow lifted to show his skepticism.

"Okay, Chris — this looks like a picture of a big sparkling boulder."

"Look *closer*," Chris said. He picked up the president's reading glasses from the end table and handed them to him.

The president put them on and held the picture closer. He stared at what he thought had been white streaks and suddenly realized what he'd missed, narrating his own discovery.

"Oh my. That looks like the skeleton of a hand. Like the bones of a human hand and maybe even an arm? What's it holding? There's a rectangular object in one of the hands; it has some writing. Hard to tell though. Um, a circle. Some lines. A cross or a plus sign? I just don't get it. Exactly what am I looking at here, Chris?"

Chris took a moment to form his answer. His fingers tapped nervously on the table edge.

"It's some type of human-like hand for sure. However, we don't know what the object is. Or the symbols. Unfortunately, the object is only readable in the 'D' photo that you're holding. The other pictures just show the fossils from different angles. We'll have some paleographers at the NSA look at this in the morning."

"They study fossils, right?" the president asked.

"No, you're thinking of paleontologists. *Paleographers* study ancient written languages. The NSA keeps a group of them on staff, just in case the bad guys try to use ancient languages to communicate with each other."

The president nodded his head. He understood.

"We'll find out if these symbols are letters or numbers. We just don't know right now, but the important thing is that they are symbols of some kind. They are not random lines."

Chris leaned toward the president, as if to reveal a secret. "Only intelligent life forms create symbols like this."

Chris shifted in his seat and continued, "These images started streaming into the branch office here in Washington, D.C. just a few hours ago. We saw something shimmering next to a very unusual stone structure, like a truncated pyramid of sorts. We drove the rover closer. This gem-encrusted boulder with the fossils was the first thing that we found. We had the Curiosity stop there and take some pictures, and the results are just amazing. This is beyond our wildest dreams."

The president stood up and walked over to the big window facing the National Mall. He stared out at the night skyline in silence, barely able to make out the silhouette of the Washington Monument. He continued to talk to Chris while facing outward.

"Are you absolutely sure this isn't some joke your engineers are playing on you?"

Chris craned his neck around to look toward the president while he spoke to him.

"It's no joke. There were five people on duty at the rover control center in Pasadena when these images started streaming in tonight. They called me right away. I told the engineers not to talk about it with anybody yet. We brought in the head of security immediately and this is officially *confidential* for now. At least, until you say otherwise. Security briefed our engineers on this, but I honestly wouldn't be surprised if they've already told their friends."

Rather than showing excitement, the president's face showed concern and puzzlement. He turned around and leaned back on the window sill. He began gnawing at his finger nail.

Chris, sensing an opportunity, spread the other three photos out on the table like playing cards.

"Here are the other photos — marked A, B, and C. These show the skeleton fossils from a few angles, but none of them show the symbols written on the object or even the building in the background. Photo D is the special one for that. However, these first few photos do show something that looks like part of a skull."

"Do you have an estimate for how old the fossils are?" the president inquired as he bit through the edge of a fingernail.

"The Curiosity has some analysis tools on board. Our guys estimate the fossils are around two or three million years old. It's a rough guess."

The president ran his hand through his receding hair to help get a grip on this avalanche of information.

"Look, I'm the president. I'm not a fossil expert. When you said fossils, I expected seashells, trilobites, or even petrified dino poop. But not this. I mean, do we even have human fossils that old here on Earth?"

"I hear what you're saying," Chris blurted out. "We do have fossils that old here, but they aren't exactly modern-looking humanoids like this one. We're simply too new."

The president lifted his coffee and took a big drink.

"So what's the next step? Are there other fossils nearby? Are you photographing those, too? What about that pyramid structure?"

The smile on Chris's face vanished. He hesitated before answering.

"We can't do any of that," Chris admitted. "Unfortunately, Curiosity stopped communicating after the pictures were sent."

"What?" the president gasped.

"We suspect that the RTG finally exhausted itself after that final data transmission."

"Okay, what's an RTG?" the confused president asked.

"Well, the Curiosity isn't like the other rovers that we've sent; it doesn't use solar panels for power. Instead, it has a tiny radio-isotope thermoelectric generator. Big words, I know, so we call them RTG's for short."

"Great, now there are *two* things I don't understand," complained the president.

"Think of the RTG as a tiny nuclear reactor that generates heat and electricity for the Curiosity. As with all nuclear power sources, RTG's eventually decay to a point where they simply stop working."

The president was stunned. He walked over and dropped into his chair.

"You mean it sent pictures of the first intelligent life we've ever encountered in the universe, and then it just died?"

Chris shrugged his shoulders and he replied, "I know. I realize it's a crazy coincidence, but it was already near its expected service life. That final transmission took a lot of power. We're lucky that we got what we got."

"I almost can't believe the unfortunate timing," the president said as his head slumped. "Well, I guess we don't have many choices available now, do we?"

"I agree, Mr. President. I agree," the NASA director said.

The president leaned forward in his chair. He put one hand on Chris's shoulder and said, "I guess we're going to Mars."

Chris nodded with a large grin.

"I was hoping you would say that. And we're going to need more than just a new machine. We need to send people. Definitely a geologist and a paleontologist."

President Jennings stared down at the photograph of the skeleton hand holding the rectangular object. He studied the precise, yet simple, symbols on it. The president smiled and started laughing out loud. Chris couldn't help but mimic with his own smile.

"So, why exactly are we laughing?" Chris asked.

The president leaned back and stared at the NASA director.

"This is really huge, Chris. I think you just saved my presidential legacy from mediocrity."

They both shared a laugh that broke the tension. The president set the photo down on the table and took another sip of coffee. He suddenly looked at the NASA director with concerned eyes.

"Chris, I *am* worried about something. I think a discovery of this magnitude might affect my voter base in, well, unpredictable ways. Some may be afraid. Some may be excited. And some, I just can't predict."

The NASA director held his hand up to pause the president.

"I get what you're saying," Chris said. "I really do. But keep in mind these aren't pictures of some smiling alien staring back at us. The culture that we found seems to be long extinct."

The president nodded in agreement.

"Yes, but what about my voters that say this will diminish the importance of humans in the world? You know, on a spiritual level?"

The president leaned toward Chris again and asked, "How about you, Chris? Are you a religious man?"

The elated look on the NASA director's face slowly changed to a more solemn expression. He gathered up the photographs on the table and glared at them, pondering the president's question.

"Yes, I am," he said. "Well, I always have been for the most part, you know? However, in *my profession*, it's useful to be quiet about such things."

Chris looked straight into the president's eyes and admitted, "But I am afraid that what we find on Mars could change everything."

CHAPTER 2

Mojave Desert
Southern California

The Sun's heat cooked the flimsy rooftop on the test station trailer. It made occasional popping sounds as it flexed. The vehicle sat parked in the middle of the Mojave Desert with wires stretching up to an ancient telephone pole — it had been there so long that the protective tar coating had completely melted off.

Two people stood in front of the trailer with their feet planted on the rock-hard dirt. Hats protected their heads from the broiling sunshine. Each held binoculars. One was a red-headed Russian woman named Tatyana. She kept switching from examining her watch to scanning the sky with her binoculars. The other was a clean-cut engineer named Tommy. He kept switching from examining his binoculars to examining Tatyana. *Flight Test Engineer* was embroidered in golden letters on his black baseball cap.

They'd only known each other for a few hours, but Tatyana had already formed the impression that this Flight Test Engineer was smart, but had subpar social skills. *After all*, Tatyana thought to herself, *he's an engineer*.

Tommy wore a white button-down shirt with a tie. The Sun and heat had caused his white shirt to show massive sweat stains. The blowing desert dust was sticking to that now; he looked like he'd used mud as a deodorant. The label on his shirt could barely be seen: *Murch Motors Corporation: Lift Happens*.

The two looked eastward toward the uniquely shaped Saddleback Mountain. They were waiting expectantly for a magical flying machine to pop up over the ridge. It was nowhere to be seen.

"To be honest ma'am, I don't understand why we haven't seen it yet," Tommy said, pressing his eyes against his binoculars. "He's been flying around out there for almost an hour."

She looked at him and said with a Russian accent, "Please. Just call me Tatyana."

Tommy nodded in agreement, nodding his binoculars too.

"Okay ma'am. Ah, crap! I mean Tatyana. I can do that."

On occasion, he caught a long glimpse of Tatyana. However, he also saw the ring on her finger and knew better. He told himself he was a good man, so he gawked politely.

Tommy followed up with the unbreakable honesty of an engineer, "Of course, I assume he hasn't crashed yet. Remember, the new Murch rocket motors are very reliable and can run nonstop for at least half a day."

His tie blew up and over his shoulder. The wind was

getting worse. Tatyana's long hair was now sticking to the sweat on her forehead.

She lowered her binoculars to wipe the hair out of her eyes. Tatyana tried hard to mask her Russian accent when she spoke, often using American lingo to help hide her native tongue. She'd been around Americans for many years and had developed an extensive vocabulary of American English, including wonderful slang. However, much to her chagrin, Tatyana couldn't completely cover up her Russian accent which used to be thick as molasses.

"Tommy, if he crashes today, then I am afraid there will be no deal. Unless the motors survive the crash. *That* would be acceptable."

"No need to worry about that ma'am, uh, Tatyana," Tommy said, attempting to calm her nerves. "The CEO of our company, Mr. Murch, is a top notch airplane pilot. He won't crash it today."

Tommy felt more comfortable on the technical side of Murch Motors Incorporated. He detested the sales side of their business where embellishment was expected. It always felt to him like he was being dishonest. His boss normally handled all sales and customer interaction. Not today, though.

The engineer in Tommy kicked into full gear, and he started to contradict his own calming attempts. "To be honest, I wish Mr. Murch would've let our test pilot demonstrate it today, but he insisted that he fly it himself to show you how safe and reliable the engines are."

Tatyana lowered her binoculars.

"Can you tell me more about how the engines can run for so long on so little fuel?"

Tommy panicked. His boss told him to avoid any specifics about how the engines worked.

"Well, I'm not supposed to discuss that much detail," Tommy said with total honesty. "Rest assured that these are the most efficient rocket engines ever designed. They are ideal for providing hover capability for lightweight vehicles."

Quietly, Tommy was terrified that the ship, his boss, and his career were all sitting in a smoking crater somewhere on the other side of Saddleback Mountain. He had told his boss that flying the ship himself was a terrible idea; he was simply not replaceable. Mr. Murch dismissed his worries by telling him, "Cemeteries are full of irreplaceable men."

Tommy was not amused.

Tatyana lifted the binoculars to her eyes again.

"Yes, I assume he is a good pilot," she said, "but he is riding the only working prototypes of the MM10 engines from Murch Motors. You can replace an arrogant CEO, but you cannot replace those engines."

She looked down at her watch. "And now I feel that he is wasting my time."

Tommy had to calm her frustration. According to his morning meeting with Mr. Murch, keeping her happy was his number one task.

"Like I said, he's not going to crash the only working prototypes of our flagship product. Don't worry, the Russian Defense Bureau will have its hands on these rockets in no time."

Three miles away, in a valley carved out by millennia of erosion, a rocket-powered hover-ship spun out of control toward the ground. Keller Murch was about to die. He was holding on for dear life, making a full conversion to religion. *Any religion.*

In prior flight testing, the prototype hover ship was sensitive to every small movement of the joystick. To fix that problem, Keller's engineers installed a special stabilization circuit in the flight control computer. During high-speed flight over the ground, this device would take his erratic joystick movements and turn them into smooth command signals. This technology would lead to a super-smooth flight, almost pleasant. He could turn it on and off by flipping a big yellow switch.

"Shazbot! They must've hooked it up backwards!" he screamed out loud.

Now, even tiny joystick movements caused the external control fins to twitch wildly, sending the hover ship spiraling out of control.

With all his strength, he tried to reach the yellow switch to turn it back off. The centrifugal forces kept him slammed down in his seat; he couldn't get to the switch. He reached into his pocket and pulled out his Blackberry, swinging it hopelessly at the switch. The ship started spinning the other way and the phone fell from his hand; it was now stuck to the floor by the spinning forces.

Keller reached into his other pocket and pulled out an iPhone. The ship was starting to buck, and he couldn't focus his eyes. He swung the iPhone and accidentally hit the bulkhead, sending a spray of glass from the cellphone.

"That'll be another two hour wait at the Apple Store."

The phone flopped out of his hands and onto the floor near the Blackberry. Looking around, he reached into his jacket and pulled out his backup Android phone.

"I am *so* Type A!"

Keller held the final cellphone tight and swung it at the switch. He missed. He swung again and hit the bulkhead, knocking the battery cover from the phone. A look of horror came across his face. With a quick squeeze, he pushed the power button on the phone. It still worked.

He reached back as far as he could and swung the phone one last time. It hit the badly wired stabilization switch, toggling it back into the off position.

The ship stopped spinning. He pulled back hard on the joystick. The vehicle pitched up and started climbing away from the valley floor.

Keller found himself skimming along the tops of the cacti with loud *boom-boom-bang-thump* sounds. They got noticeably quieter as the ship started ascending. He started to breathe normally again. After a few seconds he was high enough to see a little trailer on the other side of Saddleback Mountain.

Tatyana and Tommy heard what sounded like high-pressure air leaking from a bicycle inner tube. It was getting louder as they swiveled their heads around to locate the source. A sudden, high-pitched roaring made them drop their binoculars and cover their ears.

The prototype hover ship came racing over the trailer at nearly 100mph, tilted only slightly away from vertical. It was a white capsule with thin vertical blue stripes and large black X's all over it used for camera tracking. The MM10 engines sprayed out what looked like high-speed steam. Tatyana thought the entire hover ship looked like the nose cone from any of the classic NASA moon rockets. The MM10 motors looked like long golden bells with two placed at each of the four corners.

As the ship slowed down, the control fins moved less, but the golden bell engines began moving more.

The ship circled back around, as deafening as ever, and came to a hover about twenty yards away from the trailer. It levitated there, motionless, several feet off the ground. It was an awesome sight that didn't make sense to the brain. Things like that shouldn't float.

Tommy yelled out, "It gets me every time seeing it hover like that. And to think that it's using so little fuel. It's amazing!"

He squinted and looked at the hover ship closely. Hanging from the landing gear was a needle-filled mash of what used to be the top of a large cactus.

The vehicle started to lower and come toward them at the same time — much closer than Tommy had anticipated. The cloud of dust below was swirling wildly now with rocks and debris hitting Tatyana and Tommy in the face. Still covering their ears, they had to turn away and lean down to avoid being knocked over by the wind blast. The ship settled down onto four spring-loaded feet. The whooshing roar stopped almost immediately.

Tommy and Tatyana stood up, reluctantly uncovering their ears and wiping off the dust and debris that coated their clothing. They began walking through the short scrub-grass toward the hover ship. It was silent now except for the occasional ping and snap sounds, similar to what a car makes when turned off after a long drive. They arrived at the hover ship and waited for the main hatch door to open. They heard the noise of switches being flipped inside and the sound of a small fan turning on.

The handle on the door spun and the hatch opened. A tall, skinny man with a huge smile on his face looked out; sweat poured from his head. Keller was wearing, of all things, a business suit. He hopped out and landed superhero style with one hand down in the dirt holding him up. He stood up and clapped his hands together to wipe off the dust. Keller stuck out his hand toward Tatyana in the gesture of a handshake. He said with a smile, "*Preevyet*, Tatyana!" They shook hands.

Keller turned to Tommy and shook his hand too, saying, "*Preevyet* to you too! That means 'hello' in Russian. Wow, that was quite a ride!"

At that moment, Keller saw the top of the ancient saguaro cactus jammed into one of the landing gear struts.

He turned toward Tommy and whispered, "Do me a favor, Tommy. Get rid of that cactus on the landing gear. I think that's a ten thousand dollar fine from the Feds. We don't need any attention from them right now, okay?"

Keller turned his attention back to Tatyana.

"Hi, Tatyana. I'm glad you could make it out here today. We finally get to meet in person, right? The telephone can only do so much justice to a business transaction. It's good to meet."

"I agree, Mr. Murch. That was an impressive arrival."

"I know," he said, winking at her.

After Tommy pried off the cactus, he climbed in the ship and opened a panel that had tools in it. He began to check the vehicle and do some routine testing. He scratched at his chin when he noticed two cellphones jammed in a floor panel.

As Tommy worked, Tatyana and Keller walked back

toward the trailer. She was the first to break the silence.

"It is good to be here. I am quite amazed at the MM10 engine. Murch Motors has pulled off an engineering triumph," she said, trying to avoid stepping on the quills of a prickly pear cactus. "Is this rocket engine really as fuel efficient as you and Tommy say? Will that machine hover for hours?"

Keller thought for a moment and stopped walking to focus on his words.

"Yes, it *really* is that fuel efficient, and our newest versions run all day long. Did I ever tell you how they came to be?" he asked.

"No, you have not," she replied with genuine curiosity. "And Tommy wouldn't tell me."

Keller started using a lot of body language.

"The clever idea behind them was the product of three poor graduate students working on the concept of hypersonic plasma at Stanford. But they were spinning their wheels trying to get industry interested in their invention. I saw it. I liked it. So I bought the patent, and then I bought them. They work for me now. All I had to do was ask them if they wanted to change the world."

Keller waved his hands in the air as an exclamation point.

Tatyana looked him in the eye and said, "Right. Well, I can tell you that my clients are very interested in your engines. However, we want exclusivity on this. Nobody else can market them. So, when can we have this prototype?"

Her face lost its smile and was serious now.

"Tatyana, you and your group can buy all that we build," Keller said with almost genuine sincerity.

Tatyana looked at the hover-ship and then back at Keller.

"I am glad to hear that good news because we plan to buy your entire production. However, as we discussed on the phone, do not share this with any other institutions."

"Fair enough," Keller said, nodding his head in agreement. His fingers were crossed behind his back.

With all of the small talk done, he got to the point.

"I guess it all comes down to price."

"Yes, I suppose it does. My clients are willing to pay you ten million dollars for this prototype, and that includes all of the MM10 motors."

Keller did a small jump to avoid stepping on a cactus.

"Well, you see, it's going to cost twenty million because once I send these motors over there, your technicians will reverse engineer them just like you've always done with our military hardware."

Tatyana was taken aback with his hardball negotiation — a mix of insult and some truth. She thought for a moment.

"Fair enough," she replied without confirming his accusation.

They walked over to her car. She looked up at him with squinted eyes and said, "You'll be hearing from us soon. We will wire the payment to your corporate account first thing tomorrow. That is for the shipment of this hover vehicle, including the MM10 engines."

"You've got a deal," said Keller. They shook hands.

Tatyana pulled on the door handle to her silver BMW. It was locked. She laughed, realizing the futility of locking it out here in the middle of nowhere. With an insincere smile, Keller watched as she got in, started the engine, and drove along the dusty dirt road up and over the ridge. The brown dust cloud from her wheels drifted slowly among the cacti. She was gone.

Tommy finished his maintenance and walked through the brush over to Keller.

"Mr. Murch, everything looks good. There is still plenty of fuel on board."

"Of course! That's exactly how we designed it."

Keller stared at the dusty trail Tatyana had left behind. His marketing smile was gone.

"Thanks, Tommy. Thanks for looking after Tatyana. I wanted this demonstration to be dramatic. No. I *needed* it to be dramatic. I think we hit one out of the ballpark, don't you?"

Tommy nodded his head as he wiped some dirt from his face.

"Yes, I think it went well, Mr. Murch. I only wish we had some American companies that wanted to use our motors. Now it's just going to be used to levitate Russian military vehicles. I mean, we couldn't even meet Tatyana at the hangar. We had to hide out here in the desert like rats. It makes us look paranoid or underhanded."

"Oh, it's not paranoia," Keller replied. "I really *am* trying to hide this deal. I don't think the Feds would look too kindly on this international sale *just yet*; I've got people working on it, though. My financial needs are on a much shorter time scale than government paperwork can provide."

Keller laughed at his own words. He slapped his hand on Tommy's shoulder.

"Don't you worry about NASA, Tommy," Keller said

confidently. "They'll come around when they see these motors everywhere. We just need to make them jealous enough to realize they made a mistake."

Keller glanced down at his watch to see how much time he'd lost dealing with the badly wired switch. The watch was old and the dial had a faded blue logo for *Insane Galactic Game Technologies.* That bit of nostalgia always made him smile. He looked up and said, "It's time to head home. I'll meet you back at the hangar. Then we'll head back North."

Tommy grabbed his lunchbox from the trailer and scrambled through his warden's keychain to lock the door.

Keller walked through the desert brush back to the hover-ship. He climbed up into the cockpit and closed the door. The startup process was simple because the engines didn't use combustion. Just some switches and an old fashioned key; something insisted on by Keller himself. The rockets erupted with their deafening high-pitch whooshing sound.

Tommy sat in his pickup truck, hunched over the steering wheel and watching the rocket powered ship ascend into the sky. He accelerated the old truck out of the small parking area and drove up the winding dirt road over Saddleback Mountain.

Flying behind Tommy's truck was a hover-ship powered by the MM10 rocket engines. Today, it was piloted by a once-great millionaire, a man who was only a week away from going bankrupt and losing the company he'd poured his life savings into.

CHAPTER 3

Many books have been written about how to motivate people. They run the gamut, from achieving personal wealth to simply avoiding the loss of what we've scratched together in life. When a careful study is performed, though, it's really just about greed.

We're all greedy in some way. Scientists and engineers have a special kind of greed: an insatiable gluttony for interesting knowledge. For them, reading an encyclopedia fires off their dopamine sensors. Discovering that pumice rocks can float tickles their prefrontal cortex. Interesting facts feed them and nourish them, motivating them to do something with that knowledge. Often, it's just to prove to their buddies that they can do something better or faster, sometimes at any cost. And that is why cutting edge scientists and engineers often die poor.

However, when the rare one avoids calamity and achieves greatness, they can remember the very moment when everything clicked, or at least when the initial obsessive-compulsive spark ignited.

For Chris Tankovitch, the administrative director of NASA, that event was an unusually warm winter evening in 1986 when he witnessed a once-in-a-lifetime event. While most of his classmates were going to bed, Chris and his dad packed their cheap wobbly telescope into the trunk of the family Chevette. Chris sat in the passenger seat holding a box filled with Doritos and Coke in his lap. Reverse didn't work, so his dad had to open the door and kick forward on the ground with his foot.

Halfway down the driveway, his dad slowed the car down and turned his head toward young Chris.

"I want you to know this is a special event. Your mom is furious that I'm keeping you up this late on a school night."

"I know!" Chris said excitedly, "but this only happens every 76 years. It's either now or when I'm, like, 90 years old!"

With that, they backed out into the road and drove north out of town in silence. As time went on, they saw fewer and fewer buildings. Street signs gave way to county road signs. At the very edge of town, they passed a lonely church where one window was still illuminated from the inside.

"I wonder what that person's dealing with," his dad asked quietly.

Rare streetlights illuminated the dashboard like slow flares shot from a boat. Chris and his dad followed the directions that had been spoken to them over the home phone by the astronomy club president. Each turn took them deeper into darker and darker territory. The Chevette buzzed down the road through the inky shadows.

His dad still wore his flip-up shades from earlier in the day. He leaned his head toward Chris and blurted out, "This place is really remote. Keep your eyes open for Big Foot."

Young Chris rolled his eyes.

Finally, after what seemed like forever, they took a wide turn and saw red dots of light moving all around. Bingo.

The bright lights of the big city make it nearly impossible to see the stars. Regular flashlights have the same negative effect on your eyesight when trying to use a telescope. However, red light has no effect on night-vision sensitivity. That's why everybody at a stargazing party puts red filters on their flashlights. Chris was holding his version in the car, anticipating that night's event.

The Chevette rolled up next to some other rusty cars with Ohio license plates and stopped. Chris turned on his red flashlight while his dad pulled the telescope from the trunk. On this unseasonably warm winter night, nobody needed a jacket. They walked over to the gathering crowd, their feet crunching over the gravel. Within minutes, they set up their telescope and drank in the total blackness of the rural sky.

The club president asked everybody to gather around as he waved his hands around like a shaman. He explained that they would need nothing more than their hands to find Halley's Comet that night. To demonstrate, he climbed up on a ladder so everybody could see him; he was illuminated by a dozen red flashlight beams. From his pulpit, he delivered the instructions for viewing.

"Just raise your closed fist up above your head. Stick out your thumb and pinky towards the ends of the Big Dipper. Swivel it all around your pinky half a turn. Your thumb should be pushing on the comet."

It was just that easy.

After Chris found it once, it was impossible not to

instinctively look at it again and again. It was even more spectacular with binoculars which made the long tail really glow. The telescope was almost overkill, but he tried that, too, of course.

Maybe it was the smell of the damp winter fields. Maybe it was the excitement of seeing something so rare. Or perhaps it was the MSG-laden snacks and caffeinated Coke, but something in Chris's brain clicked that night.

The view of that Halley's Comet sky burned like a living photograph in his mind. He was keenly aware of the sound of the footsteps on the gravel, the low hum of people chatting, the sound of people laughing and telling off-color jokes that would be unthinkable three decades later.

Chris was hooked on astronomy. It would transform into an obsession with astrophysics. No other subject would top that interest for the rest of his life. From now on, Carl Sagan and Stephen Hawking would be his biggest heroes.

The grown-up version of Chris was happily rolling that memory around in his head when he got a tap on the shoulder. It was from the stage assistant in the Public Relations office at NASA.

"Hi, Director Tankovitch. We've got the teleprompter set up. The press conference is gonna start in about two minutes, okay?"

"Thank you, Jim," Chris said nervously. "Hey, can you get me a bottle of water?"

Jim raised his palms up and said, "Where's the *please*?"

He laughed, pointed his trigger finger at Chris, then disappeared past a bank of light stands.

Chris was lucky in many regards. Most men have

thinning hair by the time they've reached their mid-forties, but he didn't. Chris ran his hand through his mop of hair, trying to shake the jitters that he always got before public speaking. He couldn't remember if he'd washed it that morning — the past week had been a whirlwind of daylong meetings with Congressional members and NASA officials. However, the fossil discovery was still unannounced. Chris and the president had agreed to eventually release a few of the photographs along with some basic information.

Earlier that morning, the public relations team at NASA sent out a press release to the major news agencies containing the headline, "NASA to Announce Modest Changes to Existing Exploration Plans." Chris had purposely created a bland press announcement to make it all the more exciting when he dropped the Mars news bomb. Anything this exciting would typically require approval from the executive branch, but this was his chance to be a shining star among the scientific community.

Unbeknownst to Chris, the press suspected something was happening because the president had cancelled his regular press conference that very morning.

Chris peeked out from the side door and saw the journalists impatiently looking at their watches and checking their text messages. Most had been at the White House waiting for the president's press conference when he cancelled it; their bosses sent them here instead. Even with that, only half the chairs were filled.

Chris laughed at them for being bored. He was about to drop one of the most historically significant speeches from a public official right in their lap. It was because of this pressure that he was struggling with his opening sentence.

Perhaps a heavy, self-important and boring statement about how mankind always wanted to fly? Perhaps a funny one-liner? He thought about the most memorable opening line he'd ever heard. It was from the best man at his wedding who stood up, already drunk, and started with, "Some people say *Best Man* is just a label."

Chris shook his head. *No, I'll just go with something boring*, he thought.

He felt another tap on his shoulder. He turned around expecting to see the stage assistant with a bottle of water and said, "Thank you for the wat —"

His eyes jammed wide open. Standing there was a smiling President Daggett Jennings. Secret Service agents poured into the hallway and into the back of the NASA press room. The executive entourage had just arrived.

The president smiled as he put his hand on Chris's shoulder.

"Chris, my speech will only last five minutes or so. I would appreciate it if you would stick around to answer the follow-up questions."

Chris's mood plunged. The air had been punched out of him. Even though Chris had battled to keep the Mars planning missions funded through all the tight budget years, his old classmate was about to take all of the credit and crush his moment of glory.

Chris grasped for some words.

"Well, hang on, wait, no, see, I have my speech ready to go. Look over there, *DJ*. It's already on the teleprompter!"

Chris instantly realized his blunder of using the president's old college nickname. The president noticed it too; he was also puzzled that Chris would actually try to argue his way back into the spotlight.

"First of all, it was *DJ* back when I was cheating off your physics exams in college. I thought we already went over that. It's *Mr. President* now. And I had them turn off the teleprompter. You really shouldn't try to trump me on this, okay? I'll be reading from some notes I put on a napkin. It's not a bad speech for something I threw together on the drive over here."

The president unfolded a crumpled napkin with handwritten scribbles on it.

Chris's face wrinkled into a mild panic.

"But I'm the director of NASA!" he blurted out. "I think it should be me making this presentation."

The president's smile turned into a stern frown.

"Look Chris, you are my old friend. But managers don't make these kinds of announcements. *Presidents do.*"

They were standing behind a curtain to the side of the stage. Chris looked like a child who had just been scorned.

The press noticed that the president's personal press secretary had stepped up to the microphone. They'd been expecting to see the public relations assistant for NASA. The audience swung around in their seats to face forward. The room was now rumbling with chatter.

"Hello, ladies and gentlemen," the press secretary said. "For today's presentation, we only have two simple rules. First, no cellphones. Second, no noise. After the president is finished, he will be leaving and NASA personnel will answer your questions."

The president grabbed Chris's arm with a two-handed executive handshake. He put on his big political smile and winked.

"Cheer up, Chris. Watch how it's done."

The president walked across the front of the room to the microphone and adjusted it to his height instead of Chris's lower stature. He took a deep breath, scanned the audience and coughed once. After he set his napkin down on top of the lectern, his expression became more serious.

"On July 20, 1969, the entire world held its breath as American astronaut Neil Armstrong stepped down a ladder and put the first human footprint on the Moon. I was just a toddler at the time, but I remember that moment clearly. My mother was crying because she knew that we had reached a moment in human history where things would never be the same. We could not go back to being content with our Earth-bound lives."

The president paused for effect and drank some water from a glass.

"Here we are, almost five decades later. We've maintained that wanderlust by sending machines to Mars to find things that can amaze us and motivate us. A short while ago, one of the most important discoveries in history occurred. Although we did not find signs of current life as we had hoped, we found something just as amazing. We found evidence of previous life. Abundant life. Complex life."

He leaned down closer to the microphone.

"*Intelligent life*," his voice boomed from the speakers.

A journalist from the *Los Angeles Times* jumped out of his chair and ran toward the back of the room, trying to get the early scoop on the news. He realized that the president hadn't finished and slid to a stop to turn around. He stared at the president, caught between the urge for more information and the urge to flee.

The president noticed the interruption and took a deep breath before continuing.

"I'm going to have my office manager, Francine, hand out a packet of photographs to you. They show you what we've found," the president motioned for her to start the distribution process. "Francine, if you could, please."

She walked around the room, passing out small packets of black and white high-resolution photos. The members of the press grabbed at them. Each photo showed what looked to be shimmering rocks at first. However, closer inspection showed human-like fossils embedded in the side of a large gem-encrusted boulder. The photos were labeled A, B, and C. However, there was no photo D included in the packet. That one was still being kept secret by the president and would not be released to the press just yet.

Chris stood patiently to the side of and behind the president, putting on an effective fake smile. Even he had to admit that the president could turn on charm like a light switch. People listened. In hindsight, Chris realized it would've been inappropriate for him to give this speech.

Once the packets were all distributed, the president started up again.

"What you are looking at are photos taken by the Mars Curiosity rover, several days ago from a site called Elpmis-63A. It's in a small canyon. I'm told it is part of the Pahrump Hills outcroppings. Those things you see that look like human hand, arm, and skull fossils are believed to be from a previous... *society* for lack of a better term."

Several journalists raised their hands trying to ask the obvious question — *what else did the Curiosity rover find?* The president ignored them and continued speaking.

"The desire for mankind to explore other worlds has always been there, but we are a species that sometimes needs a little motivation, a little push. What you have in your hands is a truckload of motivation. An explosion of push. I have been in meetings with our NASA director, members of Congress, and the Pentagon all this week."

The president drank the rest of his water to prepare for his bombshell statement. The *Los Angeles Times* reporter ran out the door of the room. He thought he had his scoop, but he was about to miss the best part.

"We will be shifting some budget around and reallocating some funds, but I am here today to say that we are going to send people to Mars. Now, my advisors tell me that one year from now our planet and Mars will be unusually close in their orbits. They say this rare launch window only happens every 26 months. So, I am making a promise to the American people today. One year from now, by the end of next autumn, I propose that we put a man or woman on Mars to learn all that our ancient neighbors on the Red Planet have to teach us. I want to know what important lessons they have to share."

He coughed to clear his throat.

"Let me be clear. Before another year passes, just *before* the next presidential election, we will send astronauts to the surface of Mars and will return them safely to Earth."

Chris's eyes widened and his mouth gaped open. Several news cameras caught his unflattering reaction and would use it on the front page of tomorrow's newspapers.

The president just promised something physically impossible, and it would be Chris's job to either make it happen or fall on his sword trying. He knew that the president did this only to guarantee his coming re-election. A *reversed* October Surprise.

The president continued, "These developments are new, and we will be giving out details as we get them. Now I leave you in the competent hands of our NASA Director, Chris Tankovitch, to answer your questions. Thank you."

The president gave a confident nod to the crowd and walked directly out the side door, leaving Chris all alone at the microphone. The next thirty minutes of questioning were unpleasant for the NASA director. The press wanted all the details for this so-called one-year Mars mission.

Chris pointed to the journalist from the *New York Post* who asked the final question.

"How much planning have you had for this mission so far?"

Chris looked downward to carefully arrange his words.

"Let me answer that and a lot more. Ever since the Moon Program, we've had a small team of engineers going through scenarios with regard to a Mars mission. That team's size has fluctuated over the years, but it's always been there. They've even had test settlements in the southwestern US to study the basic ins and outs of living in such a remote location. So we've done a lot of planning already. The only catch is the travel."

"What do you mean?" the reporter asked.

"Our existing rockets have very limited fuel. This means that it takes a long time to get there. That is our greatest challenge. As far as personnel go, we have a great group of veteran astronauts from the shuttle program who would be very qualified for this mission. As the president said, things are new and still in flux. I'll have a lot more for you in the next few weeks. Thank you all for coming here today."

The press launched a battalion of questions toward Chris as he slumped off the stage and out the door. He wandered down the hallway looking for an empty room. Knocking on each door, he finally found a room that wasn't occupied. He walked in and collapsed into a sofa.

Chris was trying to get his head around all that had just happened. He missed all of the glory, but got all of the daggers. A sound of shuffling footsteps came down the hallway. Jim, the stage assistant, walked past the open door, but doubled back after he saw Chris sitting dumbfounded on the sofa.

Jim rotated his head to read the name plate next to the door jamb and said, "Oh, there you are Director... *Sally*?"

He laughed as they both realized Chris was in some random NASA employee's office.

"I'm a bit late," Jim admitted, "but here's that bottle of water that you asked for."

"Hah, yes, thank you, Jim," Chris said quietly.

Chris opened the bottle and chuckled at the absurdity of President Jennings' plan. After all, it currently took six to nine months to travel to Mars. That means it was mathematically impossible to send astronauts there and return them before the next presidential election. Well, not unless Chris could find a time machine or some kind of miracle rocket-engine that ran forever.

CHAPTER 4

News of the Mars fossils and the audacious one-year mission washed over the land like a tidal wave, steadily enveloping all aspects of daily life. Within minutes, the headline screaming across internet news sites was *"NASA Budget Goes Deep in the Red for The Red Planet."* By dinnertime, every available astronaut who owned a suit had been driven to their local TV studio to give interviews on the evening news broadcasts.

"How will this affect morale at NASA since the space shuttle program was cancelled?" asked one of the nightly news anchors. His question was directed at an astronaut dressed, uncomfortably, in an old suit with a bright blue NASA necktie. Not used to such attention, the astronaut swiveled his seat back and forth nervously as he answered.

"Frankly, it's the first bit of hope we've had in years, and I can coast really far on a little bit of hope," the astronaut said as his eyes welled up with tears.

The day before the news conference there had been almost zero chance of progress in manned space exploration. Even though we technically won the Space Race, we were now begging Russia to take our astronauts up to the International Space Station; at a cost of $70 million per crew member. After the president's new challenge, there was a volcano of hope welling up inside the ranks at NASA.

Every former astronaut secretly wanted to be on the crew picked for that mission. This resulted in each of them passively making statements about how *they* would handle it if *they* were chosen. On one of the late night talk shows, the host had invited a gaggle of Lunar Program veterans.

"So, what are the key things about this mission that make it different from your Moon landing days?" the host asked.

They looked at each other before one took the lead to answer.

"Well, they're going to need a completely new vehicle. A much larger one than the Apollo landers. Maybe even two, you know? Send one ahead that has living space plus a laboratory in it. Then, ship the crew out in another one. When they both land on the planet, they'll have room to do a lot of work. Sounds good, right?"

Another veteran chimed in.

"Yes, it's going to take several years to design and test it. I don't see how they can meet the president's schedule. And what about the travel time? It could take six, seven, maybe even more months just to get there! We don't have the rocket engines to do that in a realistic time frame."

"Several years just for the design?" the host asked.

"Yes. *Several.*"

This same crew of veterans went on to be guests for the Late Late show. After that, the Late Late Late show. Finally, they went to Taco Bell and talked about how they would jump at this mission if NASA would only ask them.

Within a few days, all of the available astronauts had used up their fifteen minutes of fame. The journalists then descended like vultures onto any available paleontologists, any professional who could even spell the word fossil would suffice. Ironically, in this case, they were hard to find. It was the fossil digging season in the southern hemisphere. Most of the experienced researchers were out in the field digging for dinosaur bones in some of the most remote locations on Earth.

NBC's nightly TV news managed to get one of Russia's most respected female paleontologists, Yeva Turoskova, on a satellite video phone from a dig in Australia. Her claim to fame was that she was also a retired cosmonaut for the former Soviet Union. Most importantly she spoke English. The journalists saw her as a triple win. On the TV screen, her face was covered in dirt and her graying hair was pulled back in a single ponytail.

The news anchor asked her, "Can you give us your thoughts on the photographs from Mars?"

"They are interesting, yes?" she said with genuine curiosity. "I haven't seen them close up yet, but they do look related to humans. We could tell a lot more if NASA could get better photographs with higher resolution."

She looked down for a moment and suddenly disappeared from camera view. When she came back up, she was holding a bucket. Yeva reached in and pulled out a sizable rock with a lizard fossil sticking out. It had very jagged teeth.

"Do you see this fossil? It is called *Rusellosaurus coheni*. I know you have never heard of it. It was an ancient swimming lizard. I know a lot about it. Why? Because I have had time to study the fossil from many angles. I can even guess what food it ate by studying its teeth. See these teeth? They are crazy teeth, yes? Probably a carnivore. When I get back to university, I look forward to exploring all of the information they are gathering from Mars."

The news anchor was bored. He tapped his note card on the table as his eyes glazed over.

"Thank you, Dr. Yeva Turoskova, speaking to us from a remote fossil dig site in Australia."

She gave a happy smile and said, "It was my pleas—," as the signal was cut off.

A large majority of the internet junk email began changing themes: from Nigerian treasury secretaries to Martian treasury secretaries and selling trip insurance to future Mars travelers.

An official Mars Real Estate Agency was started and headquartered out of Tampa, Florida. Television commercials began appearing after midnight. They were masked as science shows, but clearly selling land lots on the Red Planet. Acreage was cheap for now, so viewers were told to act quickly. Plots with a good view of Mount Sharp were already sold out.

In modern times, it didn't take long for the theme of living on Mars to infect the entertainment world too. One comedic late night host had a skit where he interviewed Martians who joked about losing all their money gambling on Vega, a star that was twenty five light years away.

"What happens on Vega stays on Vega."

The religious leaders of the time were quiet about the Mars issue at first. They were taking time to digest it because so many people trusted their opinions and their leadership. After all, they were just as fascinated by this discovery as the secular world.

A well-known philosophical blogger named Sean Josete composed a *New York Times* editorial. It was both hopeful and inspiring.

He wrote, "All life is a miracle, in my mind, regardless of what planet it lives on. I'm not amazed so much by its existence, but by how it develops from something so simple into something so wonderful and complex. Look at it this way. After an egg is fertilized, the cells start to quickly multiply and a brand new organism starts growing without any instructions at all from the parents. The microscopic DNA works like a fine craftsman, insuring that everything falls into place at precisely the right time. With that kind of perfection happening trillions of times every day here on Earth, it makes perfect sense that life is abundant throughout the cosmos. I genuinely wonder how God chooses to reveal himself to people on other worlds."

Within a week of the president's press conference, all of the interviews that could be gotten were given. The real estate plots were sold out. Most Americans felt this was an exciting mission, but the discrepancy between idealistic and realistic timelines would eventually kill much of that excitement. Budget problems would probably halt the program at some point in time. This was not a defense program. Therefore, it *was* killable.

That's how Washington, D.C. works. It would take a

steadfast president to keep the momentum going. In other words: it was completely doomed. The fossils would sit, unobserved, for another ten years until we sent yet another unmanned rover to wheel around on Mars.

While the president was announcing the discovery at the NASA press conference, there was a man out in California who was still in his pajamas, frozen like a statue and watching the president speak on television. He sat motionless in the kitchen of his beach house in Santa Cruz, near the top of the scenic Monterey Bay. This is where this man spent his extended weekends before returning to the hustle and bustle of Silicon Valley thirty miles to the north.

He had a TV remote in one hand and a spoon filled with raisin bran in the other. The only signs of life were the blinking of his eyes and the chewing of his cereal. On the television, he was watching what he believed to be the quintessential event of his life taking place.

He cringed as the journalists tried to get the NASA director to admit that his organization wasn't up to the task. He smiled when the NASA director didn't take the bait, even though everybody knew the timeline was impossible. Fortunately for NASA, this man watching from California, *Keller Murch*, could provide the missing technology today. He'd already built rockets that ran for days if not weeks.

When Keller heard the NASA director admit that the existing rocket motor technology would be the biggest challenge, raisin bran sprayed from his mouth. He threw his breakfast in the sink and ran downstairs to his six-car garage.

The floppy-haired Keller jumped into his supercharged

1968 Ford Mustang GT. He drove at nearly 120 mph from his beach house toward his office in Silicon Valley. This stretch of freeway known by the locals as *Highway 17* was one of the curviest mountain roads on the West Coast. It had a history of killing wealthy entrepreneurs who tried to navigate it too quickly while drunk with dotcom power and gin.

Halfway through the trip, the road passed through the mountain town of Scotts Valley; it's the only straight portion of the road. The two freeway exits there flew by fast for a driver commanding a high-powered sports car. The last exit always caught Keller's eye because of the Wendell's Restaurant at the bottom of the off-ramp. That was the first corporation he ever worked for.

When Keller was only 15, he lied to the Wendell's Restaurant manager about his age, so he could work. It was near his boyhood home in Elkhart, Indiana, just two blocks away from the mobile home factory which always made the lunchtime rush intense.

That job taught him everything he would need to know in the business world. *The customer wasn't always right, but they were never wrong.* After being promoted to assistant manager at the age of twenty, he married his high school sweetheart, Angie. They were a happy working couple; in those days you could make ends meet without a college degree.

Four years later their world was rocked: she was diagnosed with cancer. At that time, medicine could only prolong her life for a little while. She managed to hang on for almost a year. They were near bankruptcy when the end came. Keller was convinced that the love of his life would still be alive if he were a rich man.

Months after her passing, he knelt down in front of her grave and said, "Honey, I'm going to make you proud. I'm going to do something great with my life."

One night the following summer, his district manager came in to help with the dinner rush at the hamburger restaurant.

"Hey, Keller, you run the cash register. I'll cook the burgers, okay?"

While the district manager was flipping hamburgers, a glass vial fell out of his shirt pocket and smashed on the ground. A little mountain of white powder lay on the greasy tile floor, surrounded by shards of broken glass. The manager let out a yelp and threw the spatula onto the grill. He grabbed two customer comment cards from the front counter and dropped to the ground on his knees. He used one card to scoop the white powder onto the other card.

The district manager stood back up and glared at the line of customers. In a loathing voice he said, "Don't you *dare* judge me."

He immediately turned and walked back to the manager's office, carefully holding the white powder in the cupped cards. The customers waiting for their food stared in disbelief and abandoned their orders.

If the district manager's job was so stressful that he had to resort to drugs, Keller thought, *then maybe this wasn't such a promising career after all.* It was about time Keller changed course and lived up to the promise that he'd do something great with his life.

That's when luck struck. In addition to having a drug-using district manager, one of his coworkers was a part-time game programmer for the up-and-coming personal computer market. Keller agreed to help him market his games for a slice of the profits. They formed a company called *Insane Galactic Game Technologies.*

The games sold well through magazines and online bulletin boards; the internet was just catching on. The two entrepreneurs eventually simplified the company name to *I.G. Game Technologies.* It wasn't long before they sold the company for the insane price of $8 million; both walked away happy and carefree. This is when Keller learned that luck rarely knocks twice.

He coasted for nearly two decades on small investments and ended up slumming around the northern California town of Palo Alto; part of a region referred to as *Silicon Valley.* That's where the Googles and the Facebooks of the world got their start. He figured that a new location might bring him more luck.

Keller attended house party after house party of business people that he'd met through friends. However, he couldn't find the second break that he so desperately wanted. It dawned on Keller that *I.G. Game Technologies* might have been the high-point of his career.

On the night before he planned to abandon California, Keller decided to drink his blues away at a hipster café and bar in Palo Alto. He walked into the darkened establishment and all he could see was a swarm of illuminated white apples staring back at him. Everybody was *socializing* through their laptops. It was very quiet. Before the end of the night, though, he ran into a trio of enthusiastic grad students from Stanford. They bragged about the amazing work they were doing in their rocket laboratory. They invited him to see it for himself.

The next day he visited them at their lab in a building that appeared to have more balconies than classrooms. Every building on campus was wrapped in either evergreens or other scenic trees. Keller stood near the main entrance, astounded by the beauty of the Stanford University campus.

"Hey, Mr. Murch!" a voice yelled from the balcony above him. "Go in through the front doors, we'll meet you by the elevator."

He was led into a futuristic rocket engine laboratory buried deep inside this place called the Durand Building. Over the next few hours, the grad students demonstrated a rocket engine that used very little fuel, produced a modest amount of thrust, and ran for a long time.

The students had approached several government institutions and corporations to raise some venture capital, but they hit a brick wall. Nobody was interested. The students were told that demand wasn't there. The space industry was dead. They should focus their new technology on more *Earthly* applications.

Keller thought differently. He hired them on the spot. The three students took a leave of absence from their PhD programs. That day saw the birth of Murch Motors Incorporated. It had a total of four employees.

Those halcyon memories rattled around in Keller's brain as his Mustang raced along the freeway. Scotts Valley vanished in the rear-view mirror, and his past faded from his thoughts. Keller felt rushed like he'd never felt before. He shifted through gears like they were bowling pins to be knocked down.

"I'm driving like Steve McQueen, baby!" Keller yelled as

he roared down the road.

When he arrived at his office, Keller skidded into a handicapped parking space. He ran in without even locking the car doors. Still in his pajamas, he walked briskly through the beige hallways. Keller stopped at the office that housed the three engineers who had created his wunderkind engine. He now called the inventors his *Space Cadets*. He asked them how well their rocket technology would work in the empty vacuum of space. He asked them if it could push a ship to Mars.

They discussed the details and spent an hour running some calculations. Not only would the idea work in space, but it would work even better. The chief engineer told Keller, "The superconducting magnets would work even more efficiently in the freezing temperatures of space. It's a great way to boost rocket performance."

Keller didn't know what that meant, but he nodded his head as if he understood. Satisfied with their rough estimates, he gave them the thumbs up to modify the rocket designs for the vacuum of space.

Keller picked up the phone and called his lobbyist in Washington, D.C. Somebody answered the phone without saying anything.

It was quiet.

Keller heard a sigh.

"Hello?" Keller asked. "*Milburn*? Are you there?"

"Yes. Yes, I am. Who am I speaking with?"

"Um, this is Keller Murch. You know, the guy who pays you a ton of money to influence the Congress critters?"

"Hi, Mr. Murch. How can I help you today?"

"I need you to get me in touch with the NASA Director,

Chris Tankovitch. I have some valuable information for him. Is he in your Rolodex?"

Milburn sighed.

"Yes, but that is a very expensive card in my Rolodex, Mr. Murch. Especially after today's press conference."

Keller could taste the extortion.

"Look at it this way: I've asked you to sell my Murch Motor technology to NASA for the past two years. So far you've been a pretty worthless investment."

"Be careful, Mr. Murch. *Worthless* is a strong word. I don't like strong words. Besides, didn't I put you in touch with the Russian Defense Bureau? Have you met with them yet?"

Keller nodded instinctively. His fingers rattled on his desktop.

"Yes. Yes, you did. Look, just get me in touch with the director, and I'll make sure you are well compensated."

"How well?"

"Even *weller* than you are now."

Keller hated going through lobbyists, but he knew that high-level public servants couldn't be contacted directly by third-class millionaires like himself. Their office-entry fees were much too steep.

"I'll see what I can do. Have a good day, Mr. Murch."

That evening after dinner, Keller's phone rang. It was a Washington, D.C. area code. He took a deep breath and answered, "Hello, this is Keller Murch from the Murch Motors Corporation."

On the other end of the phone was the NASA director. He sounded defeated and exhausted.

"Hi, Mr. Murch. This is Chris Tankovitch. I've only got a minute, but our mutual friend Milburn told me you have some information that might assist in our mission to Mars?"

Keller thought hard about his next statement.

"Director Tankovitch, you don't have to worry about how you'll get the astronauts to Mars. I have the rocket engines that'll get them there in a month. I can show you a working prototype. No budget fight will kill this program."

There was silence from Chris's side of the phone. Keller could almost picture Chris doing mental calculations and schedule changes.

"You have my attention," Chris said. "I'm flying out to Arizona for some interviews over the next few days. Let's see... how about I come visit you at your place on Friday morning?"

"That'll work," Keller replied.

"Okay, I look forward to meeting you, Mr. Murch."

After they ended the phone call, Keller did a fist pump to celebrate. He felt proud, convinced that he was finally doing something great.

After Chris closed his phone, he thought to himself, *I hope this guy's for real.*

Keller picked the phone back up and dialed a very long number. He tapped his foot while the phone went through various switchboards. It finally rang with an odd European ringtone. He looked nervously at his watch trying to calculate what time it was in Russia. While the phone was ringing, he chanted, "Please don't be there, please don't be there, please don't be there."

Somebody answered.

"Hello!" Keller blurted out with surprise. "Yes, I need to speak with Tatyana. Is she available? Oh rats, then can I leave her a message? Yes. Okay. This is her old friend Keller Murch from America. Could you please tell her that I have to cancel our deal and the shipment? No hard feelings. I'll return the money in a few weeks when it's convenient for me. All right, thank you."

Unbeknownst to his employees at Murch Motors, Keller was going to coast on the ill-gotten money from the Russians until the federal contracts started rolling in from NASA, if they ever did. It was a simple plan in theory, but he'd learn more when Chris Tankovitch visited him at his home on the ocean.

CHAPTER 5

Near Monument Valley
Northern Arizona

Seventeen astronauts stood in the broiling desert sunshine. They wore prototype space suits while waiting for a gunshot. Each made eye contact with the others nearby as an unspoken acknowledgement — this was a strange and rushed interview process. Rumor had it they would run straight through the desert for two miles before the *stress* interview would begin.

In the days leading up to the president's big press conference, NASA had been secretly discussing the discovery with astronauts, mostly those with space flight experience. In the end, they found thirty-two candidates, but ten were either retired or in the process of retiring.

Due to prior commitments (like those scheduled for the International Space Station), many from the remaining talent pool couldn't make this quickly assembled interview process. Right now, only seventeen of them were standing in the late morning desert heat, waiting for that gunshot.

Two days ago, they arrived at the hotels just outside of Monument Valley to get ready for this multi-day interview process. Yesterday, they toured an existing simulated Mars habitat located deep in the desert. Earlier this morning they went through an in-depth physical along with a detailed background questionnaire. The site they were at today was near the rocky outcroppings made famous by many Old West cowboy movies. NASA chose it for its similarity to the Mars terrain.

One small part of the interview process involved seeing how the candidate's cognitive skills reacted after a stressful experience. NASA leadership wanted them to be *physically stressed* just prior to a quick interview consisting of some brain teaser questions. Jabbing them with adrenaline syringes was not an option, so they decided a long sprint through the hot desert would accomplish the same result.

The astronauts could see Chris Tankovitch talking with a small group of NASA personnel. Only a few words here and there made it to the astronauts. He must've been telling a joke because the group laughed heartily after his final words. The astronauts didn't catch it. Chris picked up his megaphone and walked out in front of the interviewees.

"Thank you all for coming here today. As you know, we are trying to select a crew for the first human mission to Mars. Each of you has a chance to make it onto that rocket. We'll be choosing two of you to make that voyage. Just getting here these past two days..." he paused and looked up and down the line of candidates.

He continued, "Just getting here to this last part of the interview process means that you are the best qualified individuals that our country has to offer. You should be proud."

Chris looked up at the Sun and wiped the sweat from his brow, lifting some papers to shield his eyes.

"When I fire off the starter pistol, I want you to run straight east through the desert as fast as you can for about two miles. We've laid out some markers for you to follow. At the end you will find a mockup of some Mars housing units. And by mockup, I mean they look nothing like the Mars housing unit that you toured yesterday. We didn't have a lot of time for this, so they're just trailers. I apologize for the crude nature of this. Just find the trailer with your name written on the door and go inside. Okay. Good luck."

The astronauts looked around one more time at their fellow interviewees standing next to them. Everybody was drenched in sweat in their suits. This was very unrealistic because the real temperature on Mars would be one hundred degrees below zero.

This is what bureaucracy on a low budget gets you, an astronaut named Adam thought. He had correctly guessed they would be put through some seemingly pointless test like this; he'd stuffed his suit with ice-filled Ziploc bags, including inside his helmet. He was comfortable. Another, named Molly, had coated her arms and legs with the ice gel bandages that athletes use. These two astronauts were ready.

Chris Tankovitch fumbled around in his jacket pockets and produced a bedraggled starter pistol. He'd borrowed it from the local high school track team. He walked over to the side to avoid getting trampled. Chris received a nod from one of the other NASA personnel and raised the pistol to the sky.

Boom!

Seventeen engineers and scientists took off running through the desert, each footstep sending up a rooster-tail of dirt. Chris laughed out loud and said to his fellow coworkers, "Have you ever seen so many nerds getting so much exercise?"

Contrary to Chris's comment, many of the astronauts had kept in good shape since the space shuttle program ended. However, they still stumbled and flopped through the desert at the pace of drunken sailors. The uneven ground and limited helmet visibility were wreaking havoc on their journey.

Within the first minute, three of them tripped over a cactus. Another fell spread-eagle into a patch of horse-crippler cactus balls, screaming out in pain. The ice-water astronaut named Adam saw the poor competitor struggling to climb out of the prickly cactus spines. He considered helping, but he assumed that getting to the test trailer quickly might be part of the test. Adam frowned as he jumped over the struggling competitor and kept running.

At the end of the sprint, the ground rose up quickly to a ridge. As the group came barreling over the top, most tumbled end over end down the hill. When all was said and done, loud groans and shrieks were heard from many of the runners, with some grabbing their backs and limping. A standby ambulance was waiting nearby.

Just beyond the bottom of the ridge were four white industrial trailers with metal steps leading up to their doors.

The vehicles were still attached to the large pickup trucks that had pulled them to this remote patch of desert.

The oldest looking trailer was located at the end of the group. The door squeaked open. Molly stuck her head in and quickly backed out to re-read the names list again, just to make sure she had it right.

"Come on in," a friendly voice invited her.

She walked in and saw a sagging banquet table. It had bent under the weight of many heavy boxes and many years. Several chairs were arranged around the table; two were occupied by NASA personnel. Molly removed her helmet and set it on the table. She flopped down into the seat, letting her brown hair fall against her shoulders.

"Nice," she said, closing her eyes and enjoying the frigid air conditioning.

Adam arrived just a few seconds later. He walked inside and saw the table and the three occupants sitting there quietly. Adam removed his helmet and a water bag fell out of it, splashing open on the floor.

"Excuse me," Adam said. "That's never happened to me before."

The NASA personnel handed out water bottles. The two astronauts chugged. They were still breathing heavily from the desert sprint.

"I don't know if cold water ever tasted this good," Molly said, looking into her bottle.

Each trailer had two NASA personnel in it. One man ran a video camera; he rarely spoke. The other one held a clipboard and was clearly in charge. Adam saw the clipboard guy's name tag and introduced himself.

"Hi, Bill. My name's Adam. It's nice to meet you."

"Nice to meet you too mister...," Bill said as he looked down at his clipboard to learn which last name belonged to an 'Adam.'

"Alston," Adam said, beating him to it. "Adam's my first name."

"Yes. Nice to meet you, Adam. You can just call me the *Clipboard Man*. It looks like you and Molly are the only people to make it to this trailer."

The cameraman pried open the window blinds and looked out to see if any others were coming.

"I doubt anybody else made it," the cameraman said. "I guess that sprint was harder than we expected. Oh well."

Clipboard Man flipped through his paperwork and pulled out a sheet with questions written on it.

"You can relax now. This is the last of the interviews — the so-called *stress* interview. Anyhow, we're doing this as a group. We didn't have time to build a real simulator, so we're going to just simulate a *situation* instead. An emergency meeting in the Mars living quarters. Understood?"

Molly and Adam looked at each other and nodded.

"So, oh yes, I forgot one thing," Clipboard Man said. "Due to regulations, I have to ask each of you a standard competency interview question first. I apologize. This is just bureaucratic policy. You first, Adam. Can you tell me why manhole covers are round?"

"What?" Adam asked, looking confused.

"It's a standard question. Please answer."

Adam looked around the room and blurted out, "I suppose it's so the manhole cover won't fall into its own hole... which is a smaller circle?"

The Clipboard Man smiled.

"That's a good answer Adam. Now for Molly."

"Okay, fire away," she said, smiling.

"You have eight basketballs. Seven of them weigh the same. One is heavier. You have an old-fashioned, teeter-totter balance scale that you can only use twice. How do you find the one ball that's heavier than the rest?"

Molly's smile turned into a frown.

"Not that I'm complaining, but, you know, that's a lot harder than Mr. Alston's question."

Clipboard Man laughed.

"Yes," he responded, "but you're a lot smarter too. You have a PhD in flight medicine, and you're a medical doctor. Mr. Alston only has degrees in geology and engineering."

Molly blushed and quickly set her mind to thinking. She stared at the table while the neurons in her brain built new pathways to answer the question.

"Okay, I've got it. Put three balls on each side of the balance. If one side of the balance drops, then the heavy ball is among that group of three. Now take two of those three balls and put them each on a scale by themselves. If they balance, then the heavy ball is the one that I didn't weigh. If one side of the balance drops, then that's the heavy ball."

Clipboard Man raised his eyebrows in surprise.

"Okay, but what if your original weighing with three balls on each side shows them all to be in balance?"

"Well, that means the heavy ball is among the two that I didn't weigh originally. It's a simple matter of putting one on each side of the balance and seeing which side of the balance drops."

"Call me impressed," Clipboard Man said. "Not even Director Tankovitch got that one right."

Clipboard Man leaned down and pulled another sheet of paper out of his briefcase. He added it to the stack of papers on his clipboard. Molly glanced out the window to see the beautiful rusty red landscape around the trailers. The dust from the running of the astronauts was still floating by.

"All right, you two," Clipboard Man said. "Now that those questions are out of the way, we can move onto the situational test." He drank some water and cleared his throat.

"Imagine that you're on Mars and you're ready to return home to Earth. However, you've just noticed that your oxygen condenser has broken. You'll run out of breathable air in two days, long before you get back to Earth. Find a solution."

Adam and Molly stared at each other, wondering who would start talking first.

The cameraman adjusted his video camera on the tripod and added, "Okay, so you're a team about to run out of oxygen and you need to discuss what you're going to do. There are no wrong answers. Go ahead."

Adam was the first to break the uncomfortable silence.

"So, Molly, it looks like we're up a fifty million mile creek without any air."

The two NASA personnel chuckled.

"But seriously, we only have oxygen for two days, right? Do we have any auxiliary oxygen tanks left over from the excursions on the planet?"

"We do," Molly responded quickly. "We have four tanks that are full. However, those will only add another day or so."

"What if we somehow tap into the oxygen fuel tanks for the rockets?" Adam asked.

The NASA personnel were feverishly taking notes like they were observing wild animals.

Molly replied, "Well, assuming we could even do that, if we used the oxygen from the fuel tanks, then we wouldn't have enough rocket thrust to get back to Earth."

"What if we got rid of every non-essential item to lighten the load?" Adam asked. "Would that decrease how much fuel and oxygen we have to use during our escape phase?"

Molly smiled, realizing what Adam was getting at.

"Yes," she said. "That would reduce our runtime on the rockets and would leave us extra oxygen. However, who knows if that would be enough to get us to Earth?"

"Okay, then perhaps we could lighten the load and use the rockets sparingly once we left Mars orbit and tap what was left in the tanks to use, you know, for us to breathe. It might not be enough to last us the entire trip, but at least we'd last longer."

"We could also dial back our oxygen use to below-standard levels," Molly suggested. "We could keep it at just above when hypoxia effects kick in. It would be like living halfway up Mt. Everest. Slightly light headed, but still conscious."

Clipboard Man nodded his head. "Yes, yes, I like what you two did there. That was clever."

He looked back at the cameraman to make sure he was still recording. The cameraman gave him a thumbs-up. Clipboard Man was happy with their answers and said, "Okay, let's move on to the next step here."

He turned to look at Adam.

"Could you please step outside for a minute? We have a

few things to discuss with Molly here. We'll invite you back in, and you two can switch places."

Adam stood up, grabbed his water bottle, and walked out the door. It slammed shut behind him. He sat on the bottom step and guzzled more water. The mid-day sunshine roasted his salt and pepper colored hair.

"Now, Molly, you were scheduled to be on the very last space shuttle launch, right?"

"That's right. I trained for over a year."

"And why weren't you on it?"

"I came down with the flu right before the launch, so I was replaced. We had a backup program for that kind of unexpected event. Somebody was always waiting in the wings."

"And how did you feel about that?"

"How did I feel about missing out on a shuttle mission? Well, I was crushed. Tragically disappointed."

"Okay, if you got sick again, would you still notify NASA personnel?"

She hesitated.

"Yes, of course," Molly said, not looking him in the eye as she answered. "I could never forgive myself for knowingly endangering the mission, especially a Mars mission."

Clipboard Man took some notes, stopped writing, and put his pencil behind his ear. The cameraman opened the door and called for Adam who walked back in and nearly fell into his chair. Molly stood up, looking tired, and wandered outside.

"Okay, Clipboard Man," Adam said with a smile. "Ask away."

"I see that you were on a space shuttle mission once back in 2008. Your wife, Connie, was in a car accident while you were up in orbit. Tell me how you handled that stress."

Adam stared at him in wonderment.

"How do you know about the accident?"

Clipboard Man saw Adam's surprised look. He leaned forward like he was going to reveal a secret and said, "I read about it in your book. It was a very interesting story."

"Ah yes, well you must've been the only person who bought that book. You know it just reached three millionth place on Amazon's best seller list? But, yes, as you say, that's true. My wife, Connie, was in a bad car accident during my shuttle mission; actually while I was performing a six-hour spacewalk."

Adam paused to collect his thoughts.

"My crew decided not to tell me about it until I got back inside the shuttle. It was serious and she still has to walk with leg braces. Sometimes with balancing crutches; kind of like short crutches that only come up to the elbow. No running or any quick movements."

"Well, Adam," Clipboard Man said, "do you think you could be on a mission lasting many months and deal with that level of stress again?"

"I'll ask her to avoid being hit by a drunk driver *again*."

Everybody laughed except Adam.

"I'd be fine," Adam confirmed. "Connie is a very strong woman. She fights that impairment every day. She still manages to take care of our kids while I go on empty book tours and give speeches to half-empty audiences at conferences. Life has been a little stressful since the space shuttle was cancelled —"

Clipboard Man interrupted, "We're getting that same message from a lot of your coworkers."

The cameraman pushed the button to stop recording while Clipboard Man was writing down more notes. Once finished writing, he looked up at Adam.

"Okay, I think that's enough. You and Molly did well. There's a bus at the other end of this line of trailers. It'll take you back to your hotel. You can leave now. Remember, don't tell anybody about today. We'll be in touch."

"Got it," Adam replied. He picked up his helmet and water bottle and walked out through the door. It slammed shut under the heavy spring. He saw Molly standing down in the trailer's shadow, drinking water.

"They said we both did well," Adam said while descending the staircase. "We can get on the bus to go home."

"Do you think we'll be chosen?" Molly asked.

"I get the feeling they're just going through the motions," Adam said as he looked up at the trailer and back at Molly. "They probably already have a team picked out. You might be one of them. Me? Not a chance."

The two astronauts walked through the dusty red soil to the bus. The last part of this entire interview process was over and it was time to go home.

CHAPTER 6

Monterey Bay
Santa Cruz, California

The director of NASA sat in a black limo. It stood still, idling in front of the entrance gate to Sunset Beach State Park. He'd flown into Silicon Valley an hour earlier and was driven down to meet Keller Murch at the entrepreneur's ocean-side house. Chris was excited to discuss the MM10 rocket-powered spaceship idea.

He followed Keller's directions and ended up at this park entry-booth located at the top of a cliff, overlooking a beach and the Pacific Ocean. Anybody wanting access to the beach had to go through the booth and pay a fee. The only exception was for people who lived in the beach houses spread out along the coastline down below.

The park attendant leaned out of her Dutch door to collect the entrance fee. Chris rolled down the window and told the park worker, *"Four nine four Las Viento Drive."*

Only six words. The park worker smiled and said, "Good morning, sir. Have a nice day." That was it. No ID required. No fee collected. Chris had said the secret code just like Keller told him. The park worker opened the gate, and the limo disappeared down a steep winding road toward the ocean.

When it reached the bottom of the hill, the limo was just below a towering cliff with houses perched at the very top. They looked like little baby birds about to fall. As Chris was driven down the road, to his right was a beautiful white sand beach leading to the Monterey Bay inlet of the Pacific Ocean.

On a map, the bay looked like a seaborne giant had punched in the coastline. As the wealth in Silicon Valley bulged, it washed down and over the Santa Cruz Mountains, starting in Los Gatos, flowing through Scotts Valley and settling here on the Monterey Bay. Chris's limo continued driving past the beach visitors, the campers, and the tents. The smell from the eucalyptus trees invaded the car.

After nearly a mile, he arrived at an enormous steel paneled gate that enveloped the entire road. Something important was hidden behind this giant barrier. The limo pulled up to the keypad. Chris lowered his window and typed in the code: 2MURCHMONEY. The motorized gate made a grinding sound as it slid open. What Chris saw made him stop blinking.

Beyond the gate was a stretch of enormous beach houses elaborately built out of rare woods and even rarer fortunes. As he drove down the lane, he ogled the Ferraris, Porsches, and even a refurbished black Ford Model T.

Near a cedar-clad beach house, the limo had to stop and

wait — a woman in a bikini hopped out of a Porsche and nearly floated across the road in front of them. She smiled at them and waved, looking as happy as a product of unimaginable privilege should be.

The road eventually dead-ended into an enormous three-story beach house. A classic green Ford Mustang was parked casually in front of it. The house had a spiral staircase that went up around a marble swordfish sculpture. The stairs ended at a redwood front door on the second floor.

On the bottom level was an enormous garage with the doors wide open. Instead of being filled with fine Italian sports cars, it contained machinery, shop equipment, and arcade games. It all seemed very out of place for this neighborhood. Aside from the limo, the only other car in sight was Keller Murch's Mustang.

A shower of sparks flew out from behind a tall red tool box in the garage. Chris climbed out of the limo and asked the driver to wait for him. He walked toward the garage.

"Hello? Mr. Murch?" Chris asked loudly.

The sparks stopped and a head popped out from behind the toolbox.

"Oh hey, you must be Mr. Tankovitch," the floating head said. "I'd shake your hand, but I'm covered in grease. I think Keller is expecting you. He's upstairs. Go on up over there, by the swordfish sculpture."

"Okay, thank you."

Chris walked up the spiral stairs and knocked on the door. It opened immediately. The bright smile of Keller Murch greeted Chris. Keller was carrying a large pile of books, but still managed to reach out and shake the NASA director's hand.

"Thanks for coming all this way! Please, come on in. Watch your step, the natural slate floor is a bit of a tripping hazard. Hey, so how was Arizona?"

"Warm and dusty," Chris answered.

"Hah, I bet." Keller said.

He led Chris to his office at the back of the house. Ironically, it had no view of the ocean. Instead, it had a view of the vertical wall of dirt behind the house. Chris saw some clods of dirt falling down. He hoped today would not be the day for the cliff to let go and bury the house.

Keller set the books down on his desk.

"Follow me," he said. "I have something to show you."

He walked quickly toward the front of the house where the sound of ocean waves got louder. Chris followed him down the hallway and saw an enormous panoramic stretch of windows overlooking the Pacific Ocean. He looked up and down the beach, seeing crested waves in every direction.

"That's an awesome view you've got," Chris said admiringly.

"No, no, that's not what I wanted to show you. Look over by the sofa," Keller said, pointing toward the living room.

Floating above the coffee table was a model of the MM10-powered hover ship. Chris thought it looked like the nose cone of a typical NASA rocket straight out of the 1960's. However, it was just hovering there with only the sound of a pressurized air-leak coming from it.

"That's a model of what I'd like to talk with you about," Keller said with a huge grin. "My company built a revolutionary rocket engine that uses very little fuel and runs for a long time. I've had that little model running all morning, hovering right there."

Keller recognized the look of awe on Chris's face. "It's like magic, isn't it?"

Chris approached the levitating model, got down on one knee and removed his glasses so he could take a closer look. All it had on the bottom were four rocket nozzles, each the size of a fingertip. They wavered back and forth in some attempt to stabilize the vehicle. It had fins sticking out the top, but those were barely moving. Chris's face suddenly formed a huge smile of childish amazement. He put his hand under the rockets to see if he could feel the exhaust. All he felt were small, but powerful, jets of air.

"How does it work?" Chris asked without looking away.

"Well, do you know how normal rocket engines work?" Keller replied.

"Yes, of course," Chris said, still focused on the hovering model. "It's the old 'throwing rocks from a canoe' idea."

"That's right," Keller agreed. "The idea behind a rocket engine is to push on something in one direction, and thanks to Sir Isaac Newton, you get pushed in the other direction. It's like sitting in a canoe and throwing heavy rocks out of it. You and your canoe get pushed in the opposite direction of the rocks."

Chris completed Keller's explanation by saying, "Yes, and all a rocket engine does is push tiny gas particles out the nozzle really fast to get the same effect. But that doesn't explain *this*. It doesn't feel like you're pushing out a lot of air at all."

Keller smiled at the obvious technical confusion.

"That's the billion dollar question," Keller said, raising his eyebrow, "and that's why you're here today. There is more to that canoe analogy. As I mentioned, you can either throw heavy rocks slowly or light rocks quickly. My company has developed a rocket engine that takes it one step further. We throw incredibly small particles out very fast, roughly a thousand times faster than a standard rocket engine. So we barely have to use any of our *rock storage,* so to speak. For the same amount of rocket fuel as a traditional engine, I can get a decent amount of thrust and run it for days, if not weeks."

"But the air coming out isn't very warm," Chris said, throwing a skeptical look at Keller. "It's not burning like a regular rocket engine."

"That's right. Nothing is burning. Each motor contains the most powerful superconducting magnets in the world. The gas is not burned. Instead, we pump electricity through the gas until it becomes an ionized plasma. At that point, the magnets push the plasma out of the nozzle at ultra-high speed —"

"Wait a second," Chris interrupted him. "You use magnets to *push* it out?"

"Yes," Keller said. "In every high school science class they teach you that moving a *copper wire* near a *magnet* causes electricity to flow through the wire. That's how a generator works, right? Well, it works in reverse too. If you pump electricity through a wire while it's *sitting* near a magnet, it causes the wire to move. Or *seawater,* or *ionized gas,* or whatever you're using to conduct the electricity instead of a wire."

"You mean like magneto-hydrodynamic propulsion?" Chris asked. "The so-called *MHD thrusters*? I thought those were all fiction."

Keller shrugged his shoulders. "No, the theory is real. It works. In our case, we're using a *plasma gas* instead of *hydro* though. That's why we call them MPD's instead of MHD's. Granted, it's not strong enough to make a sixty ton army tank fly, but certainly strong enough to push a tin-can NASA crew capsule through space for a long time. And it's a heck of a lot more powerful than any of the existing ion thrusters NASA is using right now."

Keller plopped down on the sofa after that explanation. He took a big breath and continued his hard sell.

"We have a full-flying prototype. It's so easy to fly, even I can handle it. My guys have told me that this could easily be scaled up for a trip to Mars. With a long constant acceleration, you could get to the Red Planet in about four or five weeks. The astronauts wouldn't suffer from zero gravity effects along the way and it would reduce their exposure to the solar radiation. It is truly the ideal solution to your problem."

Keller paused before hammering home his final point.

"The worst part of any vacation is getting there, right? I'm solving that problem for you."

Chris stood up and wandered over to a piano bench to sit down. He shook his head in disbelief.

Keller stood up again. He confessed, "I was going to sell this technology to a Russian contractor, but when I saw the president at the press conference with his laughable time table, I had to refocus this technology on the American efforts. Think of it as my attempt to keep our country from looking like a fool."

Chris scratched his chin, trying to find the right things to ask.

"I have so many questions," he said. "How much does it cost? How long would it take to modify it for space travel? Do you have a factory?"

"I will answer these questions in due time," Keller replied in a fatherly tone. "We'll head up to our headquarters later on and you can meet my engineers."

Keller was interrupted by the sound of soda cans being opened from a doorway at the far end of the living room. A bikini-clad brunette walked out of the kitchen, carrying a plate of food and two Cokes. Chris's jaw dropped at the sight of this mystery woman. She put the plate down on the piano and placed the drinks on coasters. On the plate were cucumber slice sandwiches with some organic tomato sauce. It seemed perfectly Californian. Chris wanted to ask Keller if beach houses were stocked full-time with beautiful women.

"It must be lunch time," Keller said. He realized an introduction was in order.

"Chris, this is my assistant, Lydia. — Lydia? This is Chris Tankovitch. He runs NASA and he's going to make me famous."

Lydia winked at Chris

"That's nice," she said. "I'll just let you boys get back to your rocket talk. Oh by the way, Keller, somebody named Tatyana called and left a voicemail for you. She sounded Russian and terrifying."

"Delete it," Keller commanded.

She walked away and Chris tried not to notice. His mind eventually wandered back to the small spaceship floating above the coffee table.

"Mr. Murch, are these motors strong enough to launch us from the ground up into orbit around Earth?"

Keller swiveled his head side to side.

"No. These rockets aren't strong enough to launch any vehicle up into orbit from Earth *or* Mars, but once in orbit, these MM10 motors would be engaged and give a nice gentle push all the way to Mars; that would greatly accelerate your vehicle. Your travel time will drop by an order of magnitude."

Chris shook his head in disbelief; it was just too good to be true.

"What's the catch?" Chris asked, squinting his eyes and looking at Keller.

Keller let out a big belly laugh.

"There is no catch," he replied.

Keller started to walk toward the kitchen and stopped. He turned around with a smile on his face.

"Well, there is one *tiny* catch — I will build these rocket motors, and maybe even the crew capsules themselves, for your Mars program. And I will only mark up the cost by one thousand percent. Given your impossible timeframe, I think you'll agree that's a bargain. However, I will only do this for you if you guarantee that I am on the *first* trip to Mars."

Ocean mist billowed through the open windows and settled on Chris's glasses. He looked over at Keller through his fogged lenses.

"You drive a hard bargain, Mr. Murch. I'll see what I can do. We have a lot of work ahead of us and very little time."

CHAPTER 7

The White House
Washington, D.C.

"What do you mean the Russians won't take us to the Space Station anymore?" President Jennings asked incredulously. He collapsed into his chair in the Oval Office, continuing his rant.

"We've been renting seats from them on the Soyuz ever since the space shuttle got axed. That's the only way to get our guys up to the International Space Station!"

"I know," Chris said.

"We're paying them $70 million a person!"

"I know."

"How are we supposed to get our people and supplies up there for the Mars mission? Why did they change their minds now?" the president asked.

During Chris's trip home from California, he received a phone call from the Russian Minister of Space Exploration. The Minister explained to him that they would no longer provide Americans access to space. Now, Chris was sitting in the Oval Office trying to explain the situation to an upset President Jennings.

"Well, it turns out that Mr. Murch made a deal with the Russian Defense Bureau to sell them his entire production of MM10 motors. However, right before he signed the contract with NASA, he backed out on the Russian deal. Oh, and he didn't bother to refund the Russians their money."

The president squeezed his eyes shut in irritation.

"It doesn't help," Chris continued, "that Mr. Murch has been on every talk show to discuss his new collaboration with NASA."

"So, the Russians are mad at one American, and for that reason, they're going to derail my entire Mars program?"

"Yes, pretty much. Except there is one compromise they've offered us."

The president's eyes shot open with hope.

"What is it?"

"They said they would reconsider if we included one Russian Cosmonaut on the Mars mission. If we do that, then they'll let us use their Soyuz rocket to get our people up to the Space Station."

The president rolled the idea around in his head. "Can we afford the extra weight of the person on this mission?"

"Yes, we can handle it," Chris said, nodding his head in agreement. "However, there is one more *tiny* problem."

"Oh, no. Another problem?" the president asked sarcastically.

"They'll let us use the Soyuz, but they won't let it launch from Russian soil."

"But what if we have a cosmonaut on board?"

"It's a bit more complicated than that," Chris explained. "The Soyuz only holds three people and if we take the extra cosmonaut, we'll have four. That's one too many. So, we'll have to modify the Soyuz and they don't want that blood on their hands if things go badly."

"Are there any *other* 'gotchas' from them?" the president asked.

"No, that's the deal they gave us. We have to include a cosmonaut *and* launch it from US soil."

"The Russians are getting on my nerves," the president said, gritting his teeth. "We may need to teach them a lesson... somehow."

Chris ignored that strange rhetorical threat. "Anyway, we'll use the Soyuz to get our astronauts up to the International Space Station, but there is still the question of getting all of our equipment and our heavy ship modules to the Space Station."

"I'm guessing that won't be the Soyuz?" the president asked, expecting to be disappointed.

"No, the Soyuz is great for lifting people, but we can't use it to lift the heavy space equipment that we're planning."

At that moment, the butler came into the room and asked the NASA director, "More coffee, sir?"

Chris waved away the offer politely.

"So, what exactly is the plan anyways?" the president asked in a curious tone.

"Well, the plan, as you know, is to make all the big launches from the International Space Station. It's too hard to send everything we need from the launch site in Florida directly to Mars. Using the Space Station as an orbiting launch platform will really help us out."

Chris looked at some notes in his hand and continued, "The mission will be made up of two vehicles, or modules as we call them. The large Science Module will be sent to Mars and stay there. That will eventually be their living habitat. Then there's the smaller Transport Module which will carry the people with extra food and water to Mars, then back home again."

"So, the two modules won't go at the same time?" the president asked.

"No, we'll send the Science Module to Mars in advance. Then we'll send the Transport Module a few weeks later with all the people and additional supplies. Again, launching from the International Space Station will really help us out on rocket fuel resources."

The president suddenly looked surprised. "I thought you said those Murch Motors were going to get us there with fuel to spare?"

"Oh, they will. The Murch Motors are good for applying a constant push for long periods of time. However, they don't have enough oomph to get the Modules off of either planet. That short launch phase will use traditional rocket engines. The Murch Motor MM10's will kick in right after the Modules leave the Space Station. Those motors will push us all the way to Mars."

"You know, Chris, that still leaves one big question. If the Soyuz is too weak to lift the Science and Transport Modules into orbit, how will we get those huge pieces of equipment from here on *Earth* up to the *Space Station*?"

"Actually, we're in luck," Chris said with a rare smile. "I had a long talk with the CEO of Whittenberg Space Launch Systems. He is willing to let us be the first official customer for their brand new Viper9 heavy lift rockets. It has nearly the same payload capacity of the Saturn V rockets used on the Apollo Moon missions. It's huge."

"Really?"

"Yes, their CEO was reluctant at first due to the high-risk nature of this mission, but I talked him into it. Patriotic duty and all. The Viper9 is a very powerful rocket; seriously, it could launch a fully loaded school bus into orbit."

"Fortunately, we aren't launching a school bus," the president said with a laugh. "I'll send a note to the Whittenberg team to thank them for saving our butts on this. I may even personally sign it. *That* should impress them."

A moment of quiet settled over the awkward conversation. Chris broke it with his final point.

"I should mention that we're having a slight *personnel* problem. The selected astronauts for our 'A team' have all declined the offer, citing safety reasons. Our backup 'B team' has said the same thing," Chris admitted.

"What *safety* reasons?" the president asked.

"They said they wouldn't feel safe flying in a ship designed and built in less than twelve months."

"I see. Are you telling me this just to complain?" the president asked accusingly.

"No, *Mr. President.* I think I have an alternate team coming together. They're a little rough around the edges, but rest assured, they are qualified for this mission. Most importantly, though, I think they can be properly *incentivized.*"

The president nodded. He understood.

"I really do appreciate the details, Chris, but when it comes down to it, I don't care *how* it all gets done. Just make it happen."

CHAPTER 8

Alston family home
Fort Worth, Texas

Adam Alston woke up every morning marveling at the fact that he wasn't dead. His life had been filled with dangerous experiences, mostly brought on by his own curiosity and stupidity. In the back of his wallet, hidden under a flap, he kept a written list of situations where he should've died. The instances tapered off after his teenage years, but every once in a while he had to take out the tattered paper and add yet another life lesson.

The memories of the first item on his list were starting to fade now, but he could never forget the upsetting details. During the first grade, Adam and his friends walked past an open field every day on the way to and from school. On the weekends, they used this field for kites and boomerangs. In September of that year, the field gave way to construction equipment. A new apartment complex began growing from the leveled dirt.

By Halloween, it had reached the stage where it looked like a collection of raw lumber in the shape of a three-story building. On the weekend after Halloween, Adam and two of his friends dared each other to sneak into the construction site and write their initials somewhere on the top floor.

When they reached the second floor, they heard mysterious thumping sounds coming from the floor above them. The entire site was supposed to be empty.

The three kids ran into the nearest unfinished apartment and stood perfectly still, far away from the stairwell. Adam, however, leaned on a two-by-four — it fell over with a loud clunk. The sounds from above stopped immediately. They heard heavy footsteps running across the ceiling and coming down the stairwell. Adam and his friends froze in complete fear. They peered out the empty window opening, trying to judge how painful a jump from the second floor would be.

A man wearing a flannel shirt and corduroy pants walked into the doorless opening of the apartment. His hair was disheveled; he was breathing heavily and he wore tennis shoes instead of construction boots. The man walked toward them while holding something behind his back.

"Hey, you kids picked the wrong day to sneak around! Get over here right now!"

Even though they were young, the kids knew that obeying his command would be a fatal decision. Young Adam leaped out of the empty window opening and landed in a construction dumpster. His wrist snapped with a sharp sprain. He was so scared that he made no sound as he rolled out of the dumpster and sprinted toward the edge of the field. He paused and looked back. His two friends had followed his lead and were not far behind. The man stood in the opening staring at them, but he turned around and disappeared back into the darkness of the unfinished apartment complex.

Adam stopped at the far edge of the field to wait for his friends to join him. They were terrified and couldn't decide what to do next. Smoke appeared from the third floor where they'd heard the sounds coming from. The three friends watched as fire consumed the top floor. They ran home when they heard the sirens coming. Adam told his parents that he hurt his wrist falling off his bike. That night, Adam took a piece of paper and started his list. The first entry said, "Lesson #1: Avoid people who wear corduroy."

That old memory raced through modern Adam's mind as his phone call with NASA progressed. He unconsciously flexed his sore wrist and ran his fingers through his short, graying hair. The conference call with NASA was a pleasant surprise; the group interview had happened several weeks earlier. It started this morning at 9:00 a.m. It was now past 10:00am, and people were still talking.

Chris Tankovitch was just one of five people on the call, but he did 90 percent of the talking. As the director of NASA, he was trying to convince Adam that he was the man to lead the Mars Mission. His name had bubbled up as an out-of-the-box thinker after the desert trailer interviews.

"Molly is also being invited," Chris added. "Honestly, she was a candidate for mission leader as well, but your shuttle experience won out."

Somebody on the conference call was clicking their pen incessantly.

"Will somebody please stop clicking that pen!" an anonymous voice yelled.

It stopped, anonymously.

Adam had written books about his space shuttle experience and his predictions for Mars exploration. These writings had made him a celebrity among the Mars Society membership. Even with that niche fame, he remained quite broke.

Although he had degrees in both aerospace engineering and geology, the one quality that NASA truly desired was his tight focus on mission safety; he had exercised it many times on the space shuttle flight back in 2008 and written about it in his book. If Adam didn't think the mission should launch, he wasn't afraid to point out exactly what was wrong and how to fix it.

Admittedly, Adam's ego already launched when he was notified about being a *possible* candidate. When NASA first contacted him to attend the desert interviews, part of that conversation involved seeing the still-confidential photos from Mars; all except Photo D.

After all of the prodding and prying had been surgically applied to Adam's ego, Chris let loose one more carrot to help him take charge of the mission.

"Adam, you are the guy," Chris said. "Think about it and get back to us. And to help you consider it, we are paying a bonus of $1 million, regardless of whether you return or not. If, God forbid you don't make it back, your family will still receive the money. Take some time. Talk to your family. Then decide. Call me either way, okay?"

The phone call ended and Adam carefully hung up the receiver. He sat there for ten minutes thinking about the mission, doodling a picture of a rocket crashing into Mars.

The future arc of his life was at stake here. Regardless of how safe the rocket would eventually be, he felt the chances of making it back home weren't good. Adam didn't take missions with risks this high; it wasn't in the nature of his grown-up self, but the monetary bonus weighed heavily on him.

After dinner that night, Adam sat out on the patio with his wife, Connie, overlooking the scrub brush fields of North Texas. They were only a mile from the school where his wife used to work before her car accident. They sat in old Adirondack chairs that were attached together at the arm rest; the red paint was bleached pink by the Sun and flaking off. The breeze still blew in warm gusts. The smell of mountain cedar filled the air.

"NASA wants me to lead the mission to Mars, but that means I'll be gone from you and the kids for a year. Maybe even more."

"Yes, but we both know your real worry is that you may never come back," Connie said, smiling gently and leaning toward Adam. "That's my only worry. My *only* worry."

She leaned back against the angled Adirondack chair. His hand found hers. Adam looked off into the distance at an old cedar tree blowing in the breeze.

"Yeah, that's about right," he said. "I want to see Cody and Catie grow up. Anything that gets in the way of that is, well, of no interest."

"No interest?" Connie said with a raised eyebrow.

She set her coffee down.

"You know, this is a big deal," she said reluctantly. "Like, a *really* big deal. You've said it yourself — nobody born *after* 1935 has ever walked on the Moon. This generation has no space heroes."

She looked out over the field and gathered her thoughts.

"Look Adam, sweetie, whoever they get to put that first foot on Mars, that person will be more famous than the Wright Brothers. They will scratch Neil Armstrong's name out of the history books and write 'Adam Alston' there instead."

She held her hands up in the air, framing the imagined text.

"And Missus Alston too? She'll be famous too?" Adam asked with a smirk.

"Hah, unlikely," she said, laughing. "But I will wave and smile in the tickertape parades. After Mars, nobody will remember the Moon landing. But if this mission is not safe on a level that you find comfortable, then don't go. If you die, then I die too. You've always said it yourself, the worst thing a Dad can do is die a foolish death while he has young kids."

"There is one more thing," Adam said sheepishly. "Regardless of whether I make it back or not, NASA will pay us a bonus of one million dollars. Hazard pay of sorts. Hah! Perhaps it's hush money."

His eyes welled up with tears. "We'll be able to call Dr. Sanders and schedule that experimental stem cell surgery on your back and get rid of those awful leg braces. You deserve it."

She leaned her head back in exasperation.

"Oh come on!" she said.

"No, no, listen," Adam interrupted her. "I'm serious about this. You could get rid of those leg braces for good."

"Get out of here...," she smirked. "You're making me sound like Tiny Tim! I'll be fine, okay? Don't do this to pay for some crazy surgery that might not work. Do this for yourself. Don't make it about me."

Adam was suddenly overwhelmed by the memory of being on the space shuttle and learning about Connie's car accident. Her lower spine was mangled. She could still walk, but not without leg braces. Since that time, she'd been raising two kids nearly all by herself. All the while, Adam pursued his career at NASA and wrote books which brought in very little money. He'd always felt guilty for not being there when the car accident happened. The only surgery that had any chance was deemed *experimental*; insurance would not pay for any of the nearly half-million dollar price tag.

Adam knew the Mars mission would be dangerous. He knew it would be tough. Regardless of what happened to him, his wife would walk again, without braces, and they would dig themselves out of their money hole. All he had to do was say yes to Chris Tankovitch.

I don't really have a choice, Adam thought.

His mild fame among engineers never translated into financial freedom. People would leaf through his books and tell him they looked interesting. Then they'd carry his *competitor's* book to the checkout line. He was a poor hero to the nerds. But now he could truly save his family and fix all their financial woes. This would be especially true if he was the *first* person to walk on Mars. It was the biggest decision of his life, and it kept him awake late into the night.

Just after midnight, he was drifting off to sleep when he felt somebody staring at him. He opened his eyes and saw a head floating just two inches above him. He jerked completely awake and yelped in fright.

"Daddy, I can't sleep."

Adam grabbed his heart to show his surprise. He sat up in bed.

"Sure thing, Champ. Let's go back to your room."

Adam got out of bed, grabbed his son Cody's hand, and walked him down the hallway to his room. He tucked him in and sat down on the floor next to the bed. This was a regular routine when his son couldn't sleep. Usually, once Cody drifted off to dreamland, Adam would sneak back to his own bed.

Instead, Cody asked, "What were you and Mommy talking about tonight about some space trip?"

Adam looked surprised.

"Oh, you heard that, huh? Yeah, it's a job I'm thinking about. That's all. It's kind of the final step in the Space Race."

Cody looked puzzled. "What's the Space Race?"

Adam searched for a good way to explain it.

"Well, think of it like this — you know how there's all that space junk up there, floating around Earth? Well, there was a time when there wasn't *anything* there. It was the unexplored frontier," Adam said, wistfully motioning his hands in the air for effect.

"I mean, there was *nothing* up there," Adam continued. "No weather satellites. No astronauts. No GPS. You had to use *paper maps* back then. Can you imagine that? Then, one night in October of 1957, there was an object floating around the Earth going *beep, beep, beep.*"

Cody leaned up on his elbow to listen. "Well, what did we launch?"

"That's the problem," Adam answered. "We didn't launch anything. The Soviets did. They launched the very first satellite. It was called Sputnik, and it floated around the Earth up in outer space, sending out a signal that basically said, '*Nah, nah nah nah nah. You can't beat us.*' They really surprised us with Sputnik."

"So that was the Space Race?" Cody questioned.

"Well, that was the start. After that, we raced to put a person in space. But we lost that battle too. The Soviets launched a guy up there first. He was named Yuri Gagarin."

"Yoo ree grug aran?" Cody said, trying to repeat the new name.

"That's pretty close!" Adam confirmed. "So, we were feeling really bad and really behind technologically."

Cody looked very curious now. He asked, "So did we ever do anything right?"

Adam patted his son on the head.

"Yes, of course we did. The Soviet guy popped up into space for one trip around the Earth and then he came back down. The year after that, we put a guy named John Glenn on a rocket and shot him so far up and so fast that he went around and around and around the Earth."

"Wow!" Cody blurted out with a huge smile on his face.

"Yeah, it was amazing. From then on, we battled with the Soviets for the next step which was putting somebody on the Moon. We did that in the summer of 1969."

"Do you remember that?" Cody asked.

Adam smiled.

"No, I wasn't born yet, unfortunately. I don't know what

it's like to watch somebody walking on the Moon. Anyhow, the Soviets were actually trying for the Moon too, but they never made it. So, we won the Space Race."

Cody looked confused and asked, "But if the Space Race is over, what was your long phone call about today? Mommy wouldn't let us go near your office."

"Well, technically I haven't decided what I'm going to do. The next step for human explorers is to visit another planet. Like Mars. And that's what I might do. Maybe."

Cody closed his eyes and said, "It sounds like you better sleep on it."

Adam laughed.

"Thanks. I think I will."

Cody closed his eyes and hugged his stuffed dragon. He drifted off to sleep. Adam was still very much awake and wandered back to his own bed.

The next morning, Adam and Connie took the kids to the park to help his son ride his bike. Cody was only a few weeks away from getting rid of his training wheels. Adam started chasing Catie around the jungle gym. Cody eventually came over to the jungle gym to join them.

"Would you guys mind if I took a trip to Mars?" Adam asked.

"Would you bring me back some Space Ice Cream?" Catie, the younger sibling, asked.

"I'll bring back a crate of it for you," Adam answered.

"Then... I guess it's okay," Catie said. "Just take some Band-Aids in case you get a booboo."

Adam walked over to the park bench where Connie was sitting. He leaned down to whisper in her ear, casually reciting a line from his favorite Robert Frost poem:

"*Two roads diverged in a yellow wood. And sorry I could not travel both —*"

"And long you stood in the dog poop?" Connie interrupted, pointing down to show him where his shoe had landed.

He laughed out loud.

"Yeah, yeah, yadda, yadda, I took the road less traveled by, and it involved dog poop."

Connie chuckled at Adam's predicament. He walked behind the bench and wiped off his shoe in the grass.

When they got home from the park, Adam dug around in his pocket for the small piece of paper with Chris Tankovitch's cell phone number on it. He took a deep breath and dialed the number.

Chris answered with his plain Midwestern accent.

"Hey, Adam. Talk to me. Do I have a mission captain?"

"Chris, let's go make the Moon landing a footnote."

CHAPTER 9

Murch Motors Production Facility
Watsonville, California

"It's 7:00am guys. Why aren't you working your butts off?" Keller Murch yelled to his team. They scattered like bugs to their desks.

The only reason this mission was going to happen on time was the combination of Keller's magic motors and the constant pressure he put on his team. Any project can come together with the proper motivation. Keller wanted to be on that first trip to Mars. He wanted it badly. If they missed the short launch window in the late summer and autumn, they would have to wait another 26 months to try again. His number one priority in life was the conversion of his motor technology from a hover ship platform to a spacecraft.

Keller needed a manufacturing facility much larger than the one he had at the Murch Motors headquarters. At first he looked for warehouse property near their existing facility in Silicon Valley. That area proved to be prohibitively expensive, thanks to the illogically funded and pre-failed startup companies that littered the tech industry. After a friend's suggestion, he looked just south of that area toward the farming region of Watsonville and found the ideal location, right off the runway at the Watsonville Airport. It proved to be ideal because it was within quick driving distance to his beach house in Santa Cruz, much more convenient than making the trek to Murch Motors headquarters up in Silicon Valley.

That part of the country also had a fairly huge pool of engineering talent available due to the heavy defense contractor presence in the area. Many of them had been set adrift after the space shuttle cancellation. Keller hired away dozens of defense workers. They would help build the space version of his rocket engines as quickly as possible. The engineers jumped at the chance to live and work by the ocean, even for the lower salaries he offered.

Large defense contractors nearby complained to the government that Keller was poaching their key engineers. The government agreed that he was poaching, but they felt the Mars trip was more important. Case closed.

Keller was so engrossed in the hectic MM10 conversion effort that all other tasks were secondary. At one point, his home phone went dead simply because he forgot to pay the bill. Keller knew how important these motors were to the entire mission; he couldn't be bothered by such pesky things as bills.

With the MM10 motor, NASA had the rocket engine technology they needed to get a crew of astronauts to Mars fast. All they needed now was a design for the two Mars-bound modules and a plan to make it happen in less than ten months.

Several contractors and government entities created the Mars Exploration Board, or MEB. The whole purpose of the MEB was to establish the goals, procedures, and module layout for the mission. Of course, Keller was the chairman, at least for a while. When the astronaut training got serious, he would have to turn over operations to his trusted flight test engineer, Tommy. Before that, Keller invited the contractors into the Mars Exploration Board for their help in brainstorming. Regardless of their input, Keller would have the last say in the design of the ship. He would constantly threaten to withhold the MM10 motors if he didn't get his way.

Weeks of meetings established the basic concept of how this adventure would officially operate. The main launch platform wouldn't be Earth. Instead, it would be the International Space Station. Starting the voyage so far out in space would minimize the impact of the fuel-hungry Earth-to-space launch phase. Just getting away from the dense atmosphere of Earth gobbled up tremendous amounts of fuel.

This plan threw some flies into the ointment. Even with the amazing lifting power of the Viper9 rocket, the Mars-bound ships would be too heavily loaded with fuel and supplies to be launched from Earth up to the orbiting International Space Station simultaneously.

Instead, all of the fuel and supplies would be sent up

ahead of time over the span of many months and many smaller launches. As big as the International Space Station was, it still wasn't big enough to hold the required extra supplies. A smaller storage capsule would be designed and permanently attached to the Space Station; it would act as an orbiting storage closet.

Keller's engineers came up with the detailed design of the smaller storage capsule. They named it the *Storage Wart* because it looked like a strange growth on the Space Station. The Science and Transport Modules, to be shipped up later, would be deemed *Big Turtle* and *Little Turtle* respectively. The "Turtle" nickname came from their faceted roof shapes covered with flat solar panels. They looked like huge, shiny, black turtle shells.

Although Keller had very smart designers working for him, their ultimate skills were not what he needed to produce the Turtles quickly. As much as he hated to do it, Keller had to contact traditional defense contractors who had experience in building lightweight robust structures.

Some of the airframe manufacturers had small independent groups to get things done much faster than their traditional counterparts. It was well known that Lockheed Martin had the Skunk Works group and Boeing had the Phantom Works group. Keller wasn't just after their ability to build complicated things quickly. He also needed to hire the big guys because they knew how to fill out all of the government paperwork, a critically important skill if you wanted to get paid.

Fortunately, he was able to team up with one of the small autonomous teams from the enormous Mayal-Maddox defense contractor. They got the ball rolling on manufacturing both Little Turtle and Big Turtle.

Without making it publicly known, they opened a manufacturing facility along the taxiway at the Watsonville Airport. The assumption was that it would make it easy to incorporate the MM10 motors if they were next door neighbors. They humorously called their secret operation The ManureWorks to reflect the aroma that sometimes flooded the region when the wind blew in from the farm fields around town.

While two-thirds of the ManureWorks team worked on the two Turtles, the other third completed the Storage Wart section of the Space Station; it was to be launched in early Spring. A few weeks after that, it would be used to house the fuel, food and other supplies until the two Turtles were lifted up into orbit.

Just prior to launching the Storage Wart up to the Space Station, the president asked for a closed-door meeting with the lead engineer on the design team.

The rather modest manager was excited to meet the president.

"Hello, Mr. President! It's an honor to meet you. I can't tell you how excited I am for this whole project."

The president gave his political, uncommitted smile.

"I think we're all excited for it. And by the way, thank you for coming here today. This meeting is to discuss a small change regarding the design of the so-called *Storage Wart*."

"But we're basically *done*," the lead engineer explained, shaking his head. "It's almost ready to be launched."

"Well, it should be a simple change. All that I need you to do is add a storage box on the outside of the Storage Wart, roughly four feet wide by twelve feet long and maybe two feet deep. I have some blueprints here from one of my Pentagon guys. Just give it a 28 Volt power source and my guys will do the rest."

The president handed a large envelope over to the engineer. He pulled out the blueprints and carefully unfolded them on the desk. He held his head as if in pain while he looked over them. He looked up at the president.

"You're asking me to add a blank box that could contain *anything*?"

"Yes. That is *one* way to look at it," the president confirmed, "but we'll let you know the exact weights and mass properties before launch."

The president could see that the lead engineer was not convinced.

"Look, in order to get this entire mission funded so quickly, we had to shift some budget away from military programs. The only tradeoff the Pentagon asked for was *this container*. My Secretary of Defense tells me that it's just a small extension of our military preparedness. That's all. I mean, it could be a radar dish for all we know! In the grand scheme of things, it's a small detail, right?"

The lead engineer was exasperated.

"But Mr. President, this could add a month to the build!" the lead engineer said, exasperated. "This might cause everything to be late. There's just not enough time to test it. We'd need to run structural analysis on it and check out all the new wire harnesses for chaffing — there's just so many potential problem points. We wouldn't have time for any of that."

"I know," the president said, nodding his head.

"However, this is a matter of national security, and I need you to do this. You love your country, right? Can you make it happen quickly?"

"Look, let me think about it. I'll talk with the team. I don't think they'll go for it. I'm sure Mr. Murch would be upset with anything that might delay the launches."

"Thank you for your time today," the president said while shaking his hand. "Please rethink your position on this. I know you'll do your best." The meeting ended.

The next day the lead engineer received a phone call from the IRS regarding some questionable deductions he'd included on his tax returns two years earlier. He was warned not to destroy any tax records or paperwork. The IRS might have to investigate even *further* back, especially during the time he'd started a small business that eventually failed. The agency was considering whether to ignore these issues or not. They might act. *They might not.*

The lead engineer scheduled an emergency meeting with Keller and convinced him that the added compartment was crucial and important enough to have the engineers work overtime and weekends. Keller agreed. The issue was never discussed after that. The IRS never called the lead engineer again.

Production went surprisingly smooth despite the special presidential favor. The mating of the MM10 rocket motors went without a hitch, thanks to the design & analysis software they were using: big names like CATIA, Pointwise, and DesignFOIL. Everything fit together like puzzle pieces. Very large and expensive puzzle pieces.

On the Ides of March, the Storage Wart sat perched atop a Viper9 heavy lift rocket. Just before sunset, it was launched up into orbit and eventually attached to the International Space Station. The Storage Wart was ready to hold all of the fuel, food and oxygen that would ultimately be transferred to the Turtles later on.

Throughout the months of March, April, and May, supply missions were being flown to the Space Station using the new Viper9 rockets from Whittenberg SLS. Everything was being tucked away in the Storage Wart.

The large Science Module, also known as the Big Turtle habitat, was mounted on a Viper9 Heavy Lifter rocket and sent up to the Space Station on Memorial Day. Once it arrived, the laborious work of transferring supplies from the Storage Wart to the Big Turtle commenced. Moving large heavy objects by hand while floating in space turned out to be cumbersome, but the Space Station staff completed the supply movement without much complaint.

The crew would have enough supplies to last them about one month. After that, they would return home.

With the Turtles utilizing the MM10 rockets after leaving planetary orbit, the trip there would take about 28 days and the trip home would take about 31 days. The difference had to do with the changes in orbit location between when they landed on Mars and when they left from Mars.

Long before any of the launches occurred, functional mockups of the Science and Transport Modules were built and located in large buildings adjacent to the Murch Motors/ManureWorks facilities. It would give the astronauts a place to train and get used to the equipment while the ManureWorks completed the flight-ready vehicles that would ultimate go into space. Later on, the mockups would be transported to the Johnson Space Center in Houston. That would allow NASA engineers to troubleshoot any potential problems using the identical ship copies. This ability to fix unforeseen problems using identical hardware had proven a life saver for the Apollo 13 crew.

At some point in time, a Russian Soyuz rocket would be sent over to Florida and installed on a one-of-a-kind launch platform, only to be used once. Since the Viper9 couldn't yet launch people into space, that task would be left up to the Soyuz rocket. For years, it had proven to be a reliable way to get crews up to the International Space Station.

Prior to the start of construction of the Turtles, though, Chris faced the task of completing his team of astronauts. After more extended interviews and searching, he finally assembled a group of motivated people. Keller got his wish to be on board. The Russians got their wish too.

CHAPTER 10

The first three members of the Mars crew mission came together quickly. Adam and Molly both accepted the challenge. Keller assumed he was included by default. The Russians demanded that NASA include a cosmonaut after Keller nixed his deal with the Russian Defense Bureau.

Chris searched far and wide to find the perfect Russian Cosmonaut. With the team now complete, he brought them together at a training facility near the Watsonville Airport. They would spend the next several months working and training together. On the night after they all arrived, Chris Tankovitch recommended that the four crewmembers have a meal together to get to know each other.

Keller arrived late, even though his beach house was literally just a few minutes away. Everybody else had already ordered their food. He sat down and opened a menu.

"How would you like your coffee, Darling?" the waitress at the Denny's in Santa Cruz asked.

Since this was to be their grand introduction to each other, Adam chose the familiar Denny's restaurant as a place to meet. He always thought it was a comfortable place to talk and share stories. Mostly, he liked the weight of the dense coffee mugs and the clunk they made on the table.

The waitress was getting impatient with Keller.

"So, how do you like your coffee?" she asked again.

He grinned at the waitress. "I like my coffee like I like my women: *caffeinated.*"

The waitress laughed and winked at Keller as she walked away. Adam stirred his coffee with a clink sound that broke the silence.

"I think this meal is the start of something great," Adam said reassuringly. "This group is going to change history."

"Well, let's not get too far ahead of ourselves," Keller blurted out. "This meal is the start of a long gastrointestinal struggle; I have a very sensitive stomach, and I don't see any organic food on this menu."

Keller was noticeably fidgety.

"It's okay," Adam said. "You don't have to eat anything. Now, I know we've all heard a little bit about each other already. I figured this would be a good place to tell the whole story. I'll tell you about myself and then we'll go around the table, okay?"

Adam looked over his glasses at everybody to see if they were in agreement.

"My name is Adam Alston, and I am still *barely* thirty-something years old. I grew up in Fort Worth, Texas. My claim to fame is that I was on the shuttle mission STS-123.

That was the shuttle mission to fix the Trelm88 satellite back in 2008. After that, I wrote a book about the mission; it sold modestly well in technical niche markets. Let's see, I have a degree in engineering and another in geology from Texas A&M. My main specialty at NASA, though, was mission safety. I'm guessing that my shuttle experience and geology degree are the main reasons NASA wanted me to lead this mission."

Yeva Turoskova was new to America and new to this group. Being Russian, she did not enjoy small talk at all. However, she was willing to oblige on this occasion. She sensed that Adam was done and nodded her head.

In her broken English, she said, "I, too, have very similar qualifications as you Adam, but my work in fossil recovery is thought to be a helpful skill here. It is funny that you mention the Trelm88 satellite. I was on the mission that launched it in the first place."

"Really? That is a small world," Adam said.

"We launched it okay. The Americans messed it up during a follow-on maintenance mission," Yeva said curtly. "Then they had to fix it on your mission in 2008. So, you broke it, you fixed it. Barely."

Adam was taken aback. "I can't comment on that. It's classified." He guzzled some ice tea and continued, "So Molly Hemphill, tell us about yourself."

Molly, naturally bubbly, said, "Sure, let's see, I graduated from the Air Force Academy with a degree in Flight Medicine and then went on for my medical degree from Indiana University. Um... I worked on the first Biosphere, and I've done years of research in life support systems for extended-length missions, just like this one. I guess that made it an easy decision for Mr. Tankovitch."

Her effervescent personality came through easily. She set her fingertips down on the table to let them know she was going to divulge something else about herself. "To be honest, I was on the fence about this mission, you know? It seems extremely risky, and I'm not the *risky* type. But I knew I'd kick myself if I said no. I've tried hard to avoid regretting anything in life. So, in this case, I had to go for it."

"You try to do what?" Keller asked as his jaw dropped.

"I want to avoid missing great opportunities. You know, I don't want to look back on life and say I coulda, shoulda, woulda."

Keller smirked. "Well, that's like saying you want to avoid learning. Regret is natural. It's just something that happens when we choose one path over another and things turn out crappy. The more regrets you have early in life, the better off your life gets later on. Believe me, I know a lot about regret."

Adam jumped in. "Okay, okay. I think she's saying that she doesn't want to waste this one-of-a-kind opportunity."

"Thank you, Adam," Molly said. "That's a good way to put it."

Keller pointed his finger at Molly.

"I gotta say, Molly, I do like your charisma."

Keller smiled and looked at each one of them. He took a big slug of coffee and continued, "Okay, my turn, I guess. Let's see... I never went to college. I ran a burger joint for years and then stumbled onto a friend who was making computer games for fun. I offered to help him turn it into a real company, and it did very well. Then we sold it for a fortune, and I tried my hand in other companies for many years. Then I started the rocket motor company called Murch Motors. I guess that makes me the least qualified person on this team, maybe even in this country."

Everybody laughed and nodded in agreement. He was very unqualified.

"But you will be riding on my vehicle, designed by my engineers, so I get to go for free. Think of me as your sugar daddy." He held up his hands to make air quotes around the word *sugar*.

Keller suddenly stood up.

"If you'll excuse me, I've gotta go see a man about a horse. Oh, if the waitress comes back, can you order me a salad with lettuce only?"

He walked into the restroom and locked the door behind him. Keller pulled a pill from his pocket and threw it into his mouth. He cupped his hands to catch water from the faucet to wash down the pill. He looked in the mirror. He was doing well.

The waitress came back with the food.

"Where's the chatty one?"

"He'll be back," Adam explained. "Don't worry. He has to come back; he's paying the bill. Oh, by the way, could you bring him a salad? Lettuce only please."

They were all digging into their food when Keller finally sauntered back to the table and sat down.

Keller saw them eating their non-organic chow.

"You like to live dangerously," he said while sitting down. "Hey, the bathroom here has one of those fancy ultra-violet hand dryers. Man, they may look like a work of art, but they also look like they'd spread the plague in a heartbeat.

Give me paper towels any day."

His barren meal arrived.

Molly finished chewing and said, "Well, you know: on the Mars spacecraft, we'll be using antibacterial reusable towels as well as those ultra-violet hand dryers. For what it's worth, research shows that they are very effective. And there is no such thing as a paper towel up there in space. Things are different in long-term habitats like that."

Keller chewed his salad and thought for a bit. When Molly wasn't looking, he stole a tater tot from her plate.

"I guess that makes sense to avoid disposable things. Every ounce of weight carried to the Space Station costs over two thousand dollars. So I guess those paper towels would cost a ton of money."

He chewed some more and asked, "You're all getting the one million dollar bonus, right?"

Everybody stopped chewing and looked around the table. They observed each other to see if anybody gave a hint that they were getting more or less. It was silent. Poker faces were on full power.

"That's not really a question," Keller said, smirking. "You are *all* getting that bonus. It was my idea. I had to make sure we had the best people here, mainly because you had to take up my slack since I'm not an engineer. I just make money magically appear. And rockets. I make them appear too. It's a skill."

Even Yeva smiled. Keller had the gift of gab. In one fell swoop, he bumped their egos and made a self-deprecating statement. He was far more skillful than he let on.

"Mr. Murch, you do not deserve to be on this mission," Yeva said. "You have not earned it like we have."

"Hang on now," Adam interjected. "Let's be diplomatic."

"Well, let's look at it this way," Keller said, spying a challenge. "With my technology, this entire mission is being planned and launched in less than a year. If you had to wait on the defense contractors alone, you'd be lucky to get a design *approved* in less than ten years. By then, you, Yeva, would be considered too old for this type of mission. Not only do I deserve to be on this rocket, but you should be thanking me."

He smiled as if he'd just won a battle, but he wasn't done.

"To be honest," he said. "This was supposed to be an American mission only. Yes, it's true. Adam, I don't think you knew that. We had to invite a Russian because I sort of shafted the Russian Defense Bureau out of $20 million in a deal that was no longer *strategic* for Murch Motors. That's one of the reasons why they weren't going to let us use the Soyuz to launch American astronauts anymore. However, they suggested Yeva, and she seems very qualified. Yeva, you are our Fast Pass to the Soyuz launch vehicle."

He made the last point by sticking a fork into another tater tot from Molly's plate.

"Now of course," Keller explained, "Adam is the team captain, so, you know, I will defer all technical decisions to him. I am just a worker bee here."

He bowed his head toward Adam.

"Thanks, Keller," Adam replied. "Let's agree that Keller has earned a spot on this mission, although in a non-traditional way. Without him, there would be no rocket engine to get us there in a reasonable time. Okay?"

Molly played with what food she had left; a thought was being tossed around in her head.

"Have any of you seen the missing photo?" she asked.

"Huh? Yes, we've seen them," Adam answered.

"No, you've seen photos A, B, and C. The paperwork said there were four photos originally, but it wasn't in the packet that I got. In fact, I haven't talked with anybody who's seen it."

Keller took a swig of coffee. "It's funny you mention that. I spoke with the NASA director about it. He told me he couldn't discuss it."

Adam looked confused. "That doesn't make any sense. It's either something wonderful or something terrible."

"You're right," Keller said, stabbing the last tater tot. "It doesn't make sense, but they probably have a good reason. Training starts tomorrow. Eat up."

CHAPTER 11

New Training Facility
Watsonville, California

"My job is to make you scream in pain!" the trainer screamed. "If your muscles aren't about to rip out of your arms and calves, then I'm not earning my insane fee! So, who's ready to start?"

The Mars mission crew all stared blankly at the physical trainer, a man who obviously ate right, exercised right, and took the right steroids.

"Don't worry," he continued. "They're making me include some team-building exercises too, but those will be few and far between. Are you ready now?"

The four astronauts cringed.

From now on the astronauts would be eating egg protein, fruits and skim milk for breakfast. No more fast food restaurants for them. Each day before lunch, they would run around the outer perimeter of the Watsonville Airport twice. The mild breeze coming from the ocean made it almost enjoyable. Depending on which direction the wind came from, though, there was the smell of either garlic or cow manure in the air. The local processing factories and farm fields could be smelly.

When the trainer was busy, Keller would sometimes lead the team-building outings. They were a mixture of hiking and jogging among amazing natural settings. The frequent afternoon excursions always involved a field trip to somewhere local and unique.

On the first outing, the crew went on a two hour hike around a state park called Nisene-Marks. Among the attractions, there were many miles of paths that curled in and around enormous groves of redwood trees. Nestled into the valleys of the Santa Cruz Mountains, it was a surreal hiking location, unlike anywhere else in America.

"This place is spooky. And where are the Ewoks?" Adam joked. He looked up at the redwood trees like tourists looked up at New York City skyscrapers.

This hike involved finding a hillside that was supposed to be the epicenter of the 1989 earthquake that struck during the World Series. The group got lost along the way, but thanks to Keller's triad of cellphones, they finally found service and navigated their way out. When walking back to the car, Molly noticed a gigantic yellow slug on the floor of the trail.

"Is that a snake?" Molly asked with excitement.

Keller smiled and said, "No, that's a banana slug — one of the largest slugs in the world."

"They just wander around here like this?" Adam asked.

"Yup, that's right. They love the foggy, cool climate here. Just like I do."

Adam picked it up and examined it.

"What a strange life form to find here on Earth," he whispered to himself. He took a picture of it with his phone and carefully set the slug back down.

They wandered back to their car and left.

It was no surprise that Keller was the most out-of-shape of all of them. The astronauts had kept up with an exercise regimen, even though they hadn't been assigned to any flight crews for several years. Keller struggled the first week, but he made it.

After hiking in the redwood park, they spent a week running along the beaches. Keller and Molly made for good running mates; they often remarked how this beach running was killing their calf muscles.

Tired of the beach running, the whole crew eventually decided to return to hiking in the redwoods. On one particularly cool morning, they left their cars at the front of the park and hiked in. After about a half mile, the dirt road became a dirt walking path. They eventually came across an old overgrown trail with a sign draped across it that said "Closed." Keller stopped and pointed at it.

"You know, we've passed by this sign like a dozen times this month."

"And it's *still* closed," Adam replied.

Keller gave a mischievous smile.

"Well, why don't we find out why it's closed?" he asked.

"You do realize we're in the spotlight right now," Adam reminded him. "Everything we do is being watched by the media."

Keller swung his head around and held his hands up.

"No media here! Who's going with me?"

Molly smiled. "I'll go."

Adam nodded to Yeva and they continued walking along the dirt path, leaving their two crewmates behind.

Keller lifted the sign up and motioned for Molly to walk under it. He bowed his head and said, "After you, ma'am."

Keller followed behind Molly. The trail went up a steep hill and vanished in dense undergrowth. They continued up and over some rocks where it popped out onto an old dirt road that straddled the mountain. It was overgrown with bright green grass and ferns. No cars had been through here in a long time.

The trail snaked even further up. They followed it, pushing the branches and weeds out of their faces. Sensing brighter and brighter sunlight, they walked until the trail emerged onto a sloped prairie that encompassed the entire top of a small mountain. The grass was golden brown and bent in the gentle breeze. They were very high up.

"Shall we continue to the top?" Molly asked.

"Of course," Keller said as they both stepped out of the woods into the prairie.

At the peak of the hill were just a few trees to break up the blanket of golden brown grass. In between the two tallest trees was a simple bench made from a split log. Keller plopped down on it. Molly sat down too. The view splayed out in front of them was of the foothills to the Santa Cruz Mountains and, beyond that, the beautiful Pacific Ocean. Far to the South, they could see the seaside town of Monterey and, to the North, they could see Santa Cruz.

"We must be able to see, maybe, thirty miles in each direction?" Keller postulated. "What do you think, Molly?"

She slid over to sit next to Keller and said, "I think this is *wonderful*."

The two of them sat there soaking up the million dollar view. Keller wondered who'd found this spot and built this simple wooden bench. He wanted to thank them.

Keller and Molly would have to leave this utopian setting eventually, but there was no need to hurry.

That night, the group had a special dinner arranged by Chris Tankovitch. He'd flown out to check on the facilities and see the progress of the Turtles. Keller volunteered his own home for the occasion, suggesting they have a campfire on the beach afterwards.

One hour before sunset, they all gathered on the balcony to have a surf & turf dinner. For Adam, it was a strange experience to sit up on such a commanding perch overlooking the ocean waves. While the astronauts ate, joggers ran up and down the beach below them. Each beach visitor glanced up to see the well-to-do people having their meal on the balcony. Adam felt farther removed from humanity here than when he was circling the Earth in the space shuttle.

Keller had one of his employees set up a campfire between the beach house and the crashing waves. After dessert, everybody grabbed a beer or wine and walked down the stairs onto the beach. The sand squished between their toes. The group walked over to the campfire and sat down, encircling the ring of flames. Keller sat between Molly and Chris.

When the conversation reached a natural lull, Chris grabbed a stick and poked the fire. He began speaking to the group.

"So, Keller tells me that the physical part of your training is going well. That's fantastic. Your training on the vehicles will start soon — the simulation modules are almost ready."

"We're actually *ahead* of schedule," Keller added.

Chris sat back and prepared to talk shop.

"Excellent. So, I'm here to brief you on a couple of things about the mission. First is the missing photo that I'm sure you're all aware of. We call it 'Photo D.' None of you have seen it and I know you're all curious. Unfortunately, it's still considered confidential because our NSA experts are trying to interpret some information in it. However, while you are en route to Mars, we will reveal it to you. Not to worry, it isn't anything dangerous. It won't make this mission any riskier than it already is."

Chris laughed at his own statement. Keller smiled. Adam grimaced.

"I also need to talk with you about *Red Hope*. Have any of you heard of that before?" Chris asked. He looked around to see if anybody acknowledged his question.

The astronauts all glanced at each other, shaking their heads.

"Okay," Chris continued. "On certain space missions in the past, one piece of equipment onboard was a vial of poison codenamed Red Hope. It's a red liquid form of cyanide. The purpose of it was in case the crew had a life-threatening disaster and would not be able to return. Our guys on Apollo 13 *almost* had to use it when it looked like their Moon mission was going to end in tragedy."

"But, I thought the onboard poison was just a myth?" Keller asked.

"Well, to the outside media and the public, it is just a myth, but we don't want our astronauts to die a horrible painful death if they can help it, right? So, if something goes wrong, the president has a speech prepared. After he finishes, your radio transmitter will be shut off for you. You won't be able to speak with anybody on Earth after that. What you do on your own, after that, is up to you. Red Hope will be on this mission."

"So, we could just use up our oxygen and die one by one?" Molly asked sarcastically.

"Yes. Or you could use the Red Hope capsules that will be with you on the Little Turtle. It's in a little locked cabinet with red and yellow stripes on it near the escape hatch door. You are not to speak with anybody about this aspect of the mission. It is top secret. Understood?" Chris asked.

The group went quiet. Nobody spoke as they took in the consequences of the NASA director's message.

"That's a bit of a downer there Director Tankovitch," Keller admitted. "How about we lighten the mood some? Everybody look out toward the ocean. The Sun is about to vanish."

The crew turned around and stared at the sliver of yellow disc sinking into the ocean. Above it, they saw bright pink and purple clouds illuminated from the dimming sunlight. The Sun was going, going — gone. They filled the rest of the night with small talk. Keller and Molly entertained each other with funny stories.

Early on, at Chris Tankovitch's request, NASA grabbed a few of the remaining structures at the Watsonville Airport and hastily converted them into pseudo-NASA buildings. Although smaller, they were modeled after some of the support facilities at NASA Johnson where astronauts usually trained. Keller and his patents had a lot of leverage over program decisions, which he wielded with joy to keep everything near his home on the beach.

After the visit from the NASA director, the crew performed less physical exercise and began using the module simulators. The Science Module, or *Big Turtle*, was very large. It contained a kitchen, sleeping quarters, and a caisson. The Little Turtle was going to transport them from Earth orbit to Mars and back again. Adam used the Little Turtle simulation module for most of his training practice. He memorized every knob and switch.

Each member of the crew practiced mating the two modules together, a procedure that would be done after both ships were on the surface of Mars. The mating process was accomplished with a pressurized extendable hallway. It stretched out like an accordion, slowly moving toward the door on the Big Turtle. Once it latched on, the astronauts would use it as a bridge between ships.

To help with small external tasks, a radio-controlled mini-rover was also included in the mission. Yeva and Adam trained on it daily.

One evening, during the last month of their training, Molly and Keller left to spend time at the beach house. Adam and Yeva went to dinner at the cafeteria. They gathered their food, sat down, and dug into their well-earned meal.

Adam paused his eating. Something was on his mind.

"Does it seem like Keller and Molly are getting awkwardly close?"

"Yes, I have seen this before," Yeva replied. "It is not good for a mission."

"As the leader of this team, I don't approve of this cohabitation they have going on."

"Then *do* something about it."

"I will," Adam replied.

He did nothing. Molly seemed to have a taming effect on Keller. Adam decided that was good for the mission.

The relationship between Molly and Keller was an open secret. The engineers at Murch Motors knew about it, and that's the way it was.

Near the end of their training in California, Keller invited the crew to a house-warming party for his assistant, Lydia. She had married well and was showing off her new house located in the hills of Los Gatos, a town known for its Lamborghini dealership and tech-titan residents. Keller thought this would be a great chance for the semi-famous crew to interact with the public in a controlled situation.

Connie had flown in to join Adam for the week, so Keller bought a large SUV to haul everybody around. On an early Saturday evening, as they drove up a long driveway leading to the hillside mansion, Keller explained how life worked there.

"Okay, so this is a new mansion built for Lydia by her nouveau riche husband. They move in higher circles than any of *you* are used to. See all the sports cars parked here? Everybody at this party has servants back home. Don't be insulted if somebody asks you to get a drink for them. Your clothes, although clean, remind them of their hired help."

Connie laughed. "If Lydia married into so much money, why does she work as your assistant?"

"Who wouldn't want to spend all day at a beach house?" Keller answered with a sly grin.

They drove past Ferraris and Porsches, parked haphazardly among the landscaped trees. On the right side of the driveway was a small vineyard used as a hobby by Lydia's husband. He got more pride out of telling strangers he was a wine maker than telling them he was a Fortune 500 CEO. They parked the SUV under a freshly transplanted, mature olive tree. The group meandered up into the house. They mingled with the dozens of strangers who wanted to meet the famous astronauts.

While Adam was getting Connie a glass of wine, a man wearing all white approached him to discuss the mission. The stranger lifted up a copy of Adam's space shuttle book and asked him to sign it. Adam beamed with pride.

"Absolutely, I'd be happy to sign it," Adam told the man.

"I bought this copy used. Got it *really* cheap," the man said as he handed the book over to Adam.

"Oh, okay. Well, thank you," Adam answered with a diminished smile. He signed the front cover and handed it back.

The stranger vanished back into the mingling crowd where he told a story that made his friends laugh.

Adam and Connie held hands and wandered through the mazelike mansion. For fun, they counted the bathrooms. So far, they'd found five of them. She was using a new pair of leg braces that allowed her to walk without the crutches, albeit awkwardly. Each room had the skin of an exotic animal lining the floors. The walls had a lot of decorative redwood burl.

They eventually pushed through some doors onto a large wooden patio overlooking the side of the mountain. Below them, they could see the tennis court and swimming pool that accessorized this mansion.

However, they were not alone. Also on the patio was a folk-music group hired to entertain at the party. The band members handed out maracas and tambourines to the guests, so they could become part of the music. Connie was the tambourine goddess for two songs.

"That was fun," she said as she handed back the instruments.

Adam and Connie stood outside overlooking the display of wealth, listening to the surreal sounds of the folk-music echo off the nearby mountain slope.

"I could live like this," Adam said.

"Where's Molly and Keller?" Connie asked.

Adam stared blankly into his drink.

"Good question. We don't ask anymore."

Adam and Connie spent the rest of the evening out on that patio avoiding the awkward guests as much as possible. The sky was full of brilliant stars. Adam pointed out which red dot was Mars.

It was now late spring. Everybody involved with the mission in California flew east to prepare for the manned launch.

This would be a first of sorts. The Russian Soyuz rocket had been transported across the Atlantic Ocean by barge. It would be launched from a remote platform near the edge of the Kennedy Space Center. This was necessary because the regular NASA launch sites were being used by the Viper9 heavy lift rockets taking supplies up to the Storage Wart on the International Space Station.

The crew arrived at the Kennedy Space Center and quickly acclimated to the pleasant Florida weather. Training continued. They felt right at home getting ready for the big launch day.

Then one of the crew members vanished.

CHAPTER 12

Kennedy Space Center
Cape Canaveral, Florida

"Where on God's green Earth is our mission leader?" Chris Tankovitch demanded. "The Soyuz crew capsule is launching in six hours!"

Unlike previous directors, he had taken a very personal role in this entire project and wanted to make absolutely sure nothing went wrong. He personally micro-managed the final physical fitness exams two days earlier, proving they were ready for the mission. However, Chris did allow the crew to relax after that milestone. Keller and Molly celebrated that night with a two hundred dollar bottle of wine they'd brought from California. All was well.

Things were not going so smoothly, however, on the morning of the launch day. Last night, all four astronauts were in their sequestered dorm rooms. This morning, Adam was gone. A panic call went out to all security personnel.

They searched the security camera recordings and found video of him going for a morning jog. He went out through the front gates and got into a minivan just after 5:30 a.m.

The rest of the crew gathered for breakfast along with Chris and tried to make things look normal for the press. One of the journalists soon yelled out, "Hey, where's the team leader?"

Chris smiled to hide his anxiety and said, "He's just sleeping in a little more. He needs his energy."

Chris was getting a mad rush of phone calls. On some, he barked orders. On others, he cowered.

Four miles away, in a lush suburban green park, a little boy was being pushed on his bicycle through the morning mist by a very proud father.

"Okay, you got it. Gotta let you go! I can't keep up!"

His voice was loud, but the echo melted into the fog.

"No, don't let go of me, Daddy!"

"I already did! It's all you, Cody!"

The little boy rode his bike, very wobbly, down the rolling grassy hill and reached the bottom. The bike slowed and he fell over sideways.

"I did it Daddy! I did it!" the boy yelled out.

Adam Alston developed an unfixable grin. He picked up Cody's bike and pushed it back up the hill. When he got to the top, he saw his wife Connie waving her arm from the bench next to the parked minivan. She held the cellphone up high, yelling a message at him through the humid morning air.

"NASA wants to know where their team leader is!"

Adam looked at his watch. The time had come.

He walked to the parking lot, one hand on the bike and the other holding Cody's hand. He paused and waited for Catie to ride her tricycle up to them. They ambled back toward the car as a group.

Adam grabbed the cellphone and put it to his ear. His wife and kids only heard one side of the conversation.

"Yeah, Adam here. Yes, I understand. No, I wouldn't want that to happen. Nobody here is showing any signs of illness. Don't worry. You won't be the laughing stock. I'm on my way."

Adam shrugged his shoulders. "It's time for me to leave. Let's head back."

They piled into the minivan and rolled out of the parking lot. The sound of crushed gravel was replaced by the surging engine, followed by absolute quiet. A red snake slithered across the desolate road, followed by a billowing cloud of fog.

The Alston family headed South onto the main road which led straight to the launch facility. After just a few minutes, they reached the main entrance guard shack. A man holding an M-16 rifle leaned over to check Adam's badge.

"Welcome back, Captain Alston. We've been wondering where you went."

The gate opened and the vehicle eased through. It followed the winding road that took them to the large limestone-clad mission prep building. This is where the families had to separate from their astronauts. Adam hugged each member of his family and whispered something to his wife; she laughed out loud. He leaned down to look into the back row of seats where the kids were sitting.

"I need you guys to take good care of your Mommy while I'm away, okay? Tell all your friends that your Daddy is on a rocket to Mars. It'll be so cool."

"Okay, Daddy, just remember the Space Ice Cream that you promised us."

Adam leaned in and hugged each one again before closing the sliding door. He waved to them through the tinted glass and walked toward the building. He disappeared through the industrial gray doors.

In just a few hours, he would no longer be an Earthling.

CHAPTER 13

The Soyuz engines ignited with a loud grinding roar; every car alarm within ten miles screamed. During the initial jolt, the astronauts looked at each other in disbelief at the ride that lay ahead. They held their breath, waiting for the launch tower to release the rattling rocket. Suddenly, it lifted and they were jammed back into their seats. Mission Control announced speeds every ten seconds. After only a minute, the rocket was travelling over one thousand miles per hour and *still accelerating*.

Subtle at first, the view outside the window showed the curvature of Earth growing by the second. The deep black of space and the brilliant blue and white of Earth created intense contrasts.

Adam was feeling nauseous.

Don't puke! Don't puke!, he thought to himself.

The rattling was slowing down. Adam turned to look at his crew. Keller gave him a thumbs-up. Yeva smiled a stressed grimace. Molly was invisible. She vomited in her helmet and it coated the visor. She wasn't flailing for help, so Adam assumed she was okay.

Aside from the nausea and vomit, the launch of the Soyuz up to the International Space Station went like clockwork. It took the better part of two days for the Soyuz capsule to catch up with the orbiting Space Station and dock with it. When the door opened, a hand reached into the ship, followed by a voice.

"Welcome to the International Space Station!" an astronaut with a Texas accent yelled.

During the next four hours, they readied the Little Turtle and double-checked all of the systems. After transferring the last of the supplies from the Storage Wart to the Little Turtle, the crew strapped in for the final leg of this two-stop flight to Mars.

The commander of the Space Station was the last to check on them. He made sure their belt restraints were all locked down. As he was about to leave the Little Turtle and lock the hatch, he spoke with the crew.

"Good luck on this mission. Wish I was going with y'all."

"You just keep those antennas pointed at our ship so we can maintain communication," Adam replied.

"Will do. Godspeed."

The commander floated back through the hatch to the safety of the International Space Station. He closed the door and started the locking procedure. A *clunk* sound finalized what their future had in store. The countdown started for the release of the Little Turtle. For thirty seconds after ignition, the traditional rocket accelerated the Little Turtle to a speed where it left Earth orbit. At that point, the roar of the rocket was replaced with the more pleasant sound of the MM10 motors which provided a gentle push that never stopped. No real noise to speak of. And that was it.

Days passed and daily calls to home were helpful with the inevitable cabin fever. Adam especially cherished his family video calls.

"It's like being in an elevator that is falling faster than it should," he would tell them, "but not *quite fast enough* for me to start floating."

Adam was talking directly to the iPad video conferencing software. On the other end of this video call was his family. They were very excited to get their daily 15 minute call to Dad on the Little Turtle. The astronauts were hurtling through space towards Mars. As of today, they were far enough out for there to be a twenty second delay between when Adam spoke and when he would hear a reply.

Adam's daughter Catie laughed and asked, "But I thought you floated in spaceships?"

Adam grinned proudly. "Normally that's true, but this spaceship is special. The motors never shut off. They just keep pushing, making us go faster every second. It's just enough to keep us planted against the floor of the ship. It's like walking on Earth if you barely weighed a few pounds. The launch from Earth to the International Space Station went great aside from me and Molly getting motion sickness. The launch from the Space Station toward Mars was a snap."

Over the next twenty seconds, Adam's message would travel from their long-range antenna through the inky blackness of space to the antenna on the Space Station. At that point it would be relayed to Mission Control in Houston.

A return message would take a similar length of time, but the time lag would get longer and longer as the mission continued. When Mars is closest to Earth, called *perihelic opposition*, the best-case round-trip communication time was only about seven minutes. Once they were on Mars, though, due to the planets having moved some distance apart, it would take a full ten minutes or more for the communications round trip (five-plus minutes each way). The longer they stayed, the longer that round trip took. When the two planets are farthest apart, that same round-trip communication can take almost 44 minutes. Radio waves move very fast, but Mars is *very* far away.

"Okay Dad, we're going to the park after this call. We'll talk with you tomorrow," Cody announced.

Adam looked down briefly, then back at the screen.

"Okay guys. I'll talk with you all tomorrow. Love you."

The screen went blank.

Adam closed his eyes for a few seconds and thought of being home. Then he thought about the million dollar bonus and put on a fake smile. He put the iPad back in the cabinet.

The small amount of fake gravity they were feeling due to the MM10 rockets altered the way Little Turtle was designed. On the space shuttle, there were panels, controls and knobs everywhere because the occupants were always floating and could reach them at any time. If the astronauts were near the floor, they could push off and float to the ceiling. The Space Station was similar in that way, too.

Little Turtle was arranged more like a ship on Earth. There were still controls on the ceiling and walls, but nothing on the floor because they were still walking on it, albeit lightly. To make sure the crew could reach the ceiling knobs, it was lowered to only six feet above the floor — taller than any of the astronauts. Little Turtle was a very cramped workspace that could've been designed by Frank Lloyd Wright.

The only noticeable noise on Little Turtle was the hissing that was being transmitted by the MM10 rocket engines through the structure and into the cabin. The Moon and the Earth looked to be about the same size now, but both were behind them. Mars still looked like a red dot far away.

Adam stuck his head up into the upper flight deck control room and commanded, "Okay folks, it's 9:00 a.m. Let's take care of the morning checklists." He climbed back down the short ladder, grabbed his checklist, started pushing buttons, and turning knobs.

Molly was already checking the oxygen supply and carbon dioxide filters. After that, she would check the food supply for any signs of spoilage or damage. Yeva was looking at the chemical supplies that would be used during the exploration phase. It included some acids and other volatile substances that needed human tending.

Keller was still sitting in the command chair in the upper room.

After the checklists were done, the crew hung them back up on their Velcro hooks and started preparing lunch. Although they had some fake gravity, they still ate typical space food as a cost savings. It was the normal stuff. Mashed potatoes, pureed steak, etc. all squeezed out of tubes or bags. Adam opened the storable table and sat down next to it. Molly and Yeva joined him. As they ate, Molly said, "Adam, tell us one of your stories where you almost died."

"Hmmm, a challenge," he said as he took a bite of the steak puree, instinctively chewing even though that wasn't necessary.

"Did I ever tell you about the time I got hit in the becuzzif?"

The two women looked at each other and smiled.

"No, you did not," Yeva said.

"Well, there was this time... Wait, hey Keller! Are you coming down here to eat or what?"

"I'll be there in a minute. Just finishing up," Keller said as he sat in his chair, shaking.

Adam returned to his story. "Okay, so when my friends and I were in high school, we were hired by a farmer to remove some large rocks from a newly ploughed section of his field. So we got some shovels and pry bars and went to work."

He looked at them to see their anticipation. He took another drink of steak.

"So we removed all the rocks except for a huge one," he said as he lifted up his arms to show how big it was.

"I put my shovel under the edge of that rock and pried and pried. It wasn't budging, so I put the shovel all the way under it, and the handle was sticking out, you know, like at a 45 degree angle? The plan was to jump up on the shovel handle. Well, I jumped, and I did get onto it, except once it flexed down to the ground, my feet slid off, and it came up and smacked me right in the testicles. Can I say testicles?"

Molly was laughing so hard that liquid steak sprayed out of her nose. Adam grabbed Molly's shoulder and asked laughingly, "You're not going to puke, are you? You look a little green!"

She laughed even harder.

"So anyway, it hurt so bad. I was sure I broke my pelvis, and there was probably blood involved. I yanked down my shorts and asked if my becuzzif was bleeding."

Adam was laughing himself now.

"So my friends are all on the ground laughing, and one says, 'No, but my eyes are bleeding from laughing so hard'."

Yeva was laughing quietly and asked, "So what is a becuzzif?"

"It's called that 'becuzzif' it wasn't there, my guts would fall out the bottom."

Yeva started to laugh out loud now, too.

Some rustling noises came in from above. Keller climbed down the stairs and, without saying anything, he rushed into the latrine and shut the door. They heard the rattling sound of a pill bottle followed by the sound of the vacuum-powered sink.

After a few minutes, the door opened and a relaxed Keller emerged.

"Come join us for lunch," Adam commanded.

"Oh, I'm not hungry just yet."

Adam looked at Keller and saw he was covered in sweat.

"Are you feeling okay? What's going on?" Adam asked.

Keller didn't say a word and walked toward the short ladder to climb upstairs. He got to the second rung before a prescription bottle fell out of his pocket. He tried to grab it, but his hand knocked it away. It slowly flew across the room heading toward the floor. When it hit, the lid popped off and pills sprayed everywhere.

Keller's eyes went wide open. The ladies didn't know

what to think. Adam lurched for the bottle, but Keller pushed off the wall with his feet and reached it first. Adam tried to grab it from Keller's hand. A struggle ensued as each tried to grab the bottle from each other. Finally, Keller punched Adam in the stomach, wrenched the bottle away, and ran over to the ladder. He stood still, breathing heavily.

"We have to collect all of those pills," Keller said with zero emotion.

Adam was still hunched over trying to catch his breath.

"What is wrong with you! What's going on? You've been squirrelly ever since we left Earth!"

Keller squeezed his eyes shut to think.

"Let's just say that I have extreme claustrophobia, okay? This medicine helps when I need it. Being in this ship though... I need it constantly. Look at this place, I keep hitting my head on these short ceilings! I tried to go without it, but that didn't work. If we find all the spilled pills, then I might have just enough for the trip there and the trip home. Without them, well, it'll be bad for everybody. You might throw me out the escape hatch."

Adam was still filled with anger, catching his breath.

"You pick up all those pills yourself. Why didn't you tell us about this before we even started the mission?" he demanded.

"Well the medical team said it was okay, as long as I only used them *occasionally*."

Adams eyes bulged.

"But you've got enough to tranquilize an elephant!"

Keller shrugged his shoulders.

"Not everybody has the same definition of *occasional*."

Molly moved toward Keller to talk with him about this,

but stopped short.

Keller walked back across the room and meticulously picked up each pill, dropping it in the bottle. Molly joined him. She noticed that several had fallen through the cracks in the floor panels and couldn't be retrieved. She said nothing. When they'd found all of the visible pills that could be picked up, Keller tightened the lid and stood up to talk.

"Look, if I would've told you guys about this before, you would've booted me off this mission."

"You're right," Adam said, having finally calmed down. "But you're here now. Do you have enough to last?"

Keller paused; he noticed that the bottle was less full.

"Possibly. I'll go upstairs and get to my checklist."

Keller climbed up the ladder and started his morning checklist in seclusion, albeit a few hours late.

In just one hour, the crew would have a classified video conference with the head of NASA. Chris Tankovitch would finally reveal Photo D and tell them what it meant to both the mission and mankind.

CHAPTER 14

"Can you hear me?" the shaking image of Chris Tankovitch said on an iPad screen. It sat on a table inside the Little Turtle as the spacecraft raced toward Mars. The astronauts were gathered in front of the screen.

"Yes, we can hear you fine," Adam responded. "The picture's kind of blurry right now though."

The crew would have to wait another ninety seconds to get a reply.

"Okay, hang on," Chris eventually said. "We're making some adjustments." He walked out of frame for a while and came back holding a Coke. He started tinkering with something near his camera lens. Suddenly, Chris was in sharp focus.

He looked into the camera and said, "Okay, this time delay is going to make this tricky, so I'm going to talk for two minutes, and then you can talk for two minutes."

Chris reached down to his table and pulled a photograph out of an envelope. "Guys, to the left of your upper escape hatch door is a locked pink cabinet. I'm going to unlock it right now, remotely."

The astronauts could see Chris typing a code onto a console on his desk. They heard an audible *clunk* sound come from the command room above them. Keller scurried up the ladder and came back down with a big brown envelope. He opened it and pulled out the stack of photos.

Chris continued with his two minute talk.

"You've seen most of these already, but you haven't seen Photo D. That is the most important image, and it will guide this entire mission. This is the photo I showed the president last year that caused this entire Mars mission to become a reality. What you're looking at is a fossilized hand — it's holding what we believe to be a granite slab the size of a credit card. On that slab are some symbols. A vertical line followed by a circle and then another vertical line."

Keller laughed under his breath and said, "So their 'LOL' took two million years to get to us? Okay, I guess *my* cellphone plan *isn't* the worst after all."

Chris didn't hear Keller due to the time delay, so he continued right along. "At first, we believed these to be a number sequence, but note that there is a third vertical line inside the circle. And if you look closer, there is a small horizontal mark on that vertical line inside the circle. It looks like a tall cross. I'll give you a minute to soak these in."

The astronauts stared intently at the photo.

"It's Calvary," Adam whispered.

"You mean... like with the bugles and the horses?" Keller asked in a confused tone.

"No, no, no; you're thinking of the *cavalry*," Adam said, correcting Keller. "I'm talking about *Calvary*. Didn't you guys ever go to Sunday school?"

The others stared blankly at Adam.

Adam didn't want to trot out his conservative Southern upbringing, but he decided now was a good time to explain.

"Okay, so there's a hill outside of Jerusalem where Jesus was crucified. It's called *Calvary*. There were two other guys crucified next to him. One on his left and one on his right. I don't know what the circle means on *this* thing, but this symbol, with the three vertical lines, is very similar to what's used to represent Calvary nowadays. Normally, it's just three crosses, though. You see it along the side of freeways a lot, you know? Three crosses next to each other? These carvings in the granite, though, are missing the two horizontal bars on the side crosses. It doesn't make sense. And anyways, how would Martians from millions of years ago know about *our* religious symbols?"

After a long delay, Chris started up again.

"Adam, I admit that's what I thought, too. I was convinced I was having a religious moment. However, if you look closely you will see that all three of the vertical lines are the same length as the diameter of that circle. The top bar on that middle cross is really short, roughly fourteen percent of the length of the vertical lines."

"Could it be *Pi*?" Yeva asked. There was a long silence as the message went to Earth and Chris replied.

"Yes, Yeva, excellent conclusion. We think so," Chris admitted. "If you wanted to prove to some future explorer that you were an advanced culture, then you might present some example of advanced thinking. Like 'the Sun is round' or then you might tell the future travelers that you're familiar with the number Pi. If you know about Pi, then your math system is very advanced."

"Okay, I don't quite understand," Keller admitted. "I consider myself pretty tech savvy, but I slept through geometry class. What is *Pi* again? Why is it important?"

Adam thought for a moment and explained, "Well, no matter how big a circle is, if you wrap a string around the outside of it once, and then unwind that string into a straight line, the length of it will always be equal to about 3.14 times the width of the circle. It works for *any* circle of *any* size."

"And?" Keller said, looking unimpressed.

"And it is absolutely crucial for advanced math," Yeva chimed in. "The kind of math that gets you launched off the Earth in rocket ships. You cannot leave your planet without knowing about the number Pi."

Keller was suddenly overcome with regret about sleeping through high school geometry. He blurted out, "Look who was paying attention in math class!"

Silence. Lots and lots of silence.

"We believe," Chris continued, "this granite slab with symbols was meant as a calling card to say, '*We know our stuff — pay attention to us.*' However, we are really interested in what's shown in the *background* of the picture."

The astronauts looked closely and could see a pyramid-like structure with a circular door on it. It wasn't very large, but it all seemed to be made out of granite or smooth rock of some type.

"After you land and establish your living quarters on Mars, we'll have you take some better photos of the fossils. However, after that, we'd like you to focus on that pyramid structure. We want to know what is behind that door."

Keller smirked. "So do you think we're going to find

little green men behind door number one?"

A minute and half later, Chris came back with, "Probably not. Oh, there is one more thing. A few days after our NSA experts analyzed the photos, they found that the round door on the pyramid structure actually has a symbol carved on it, too. It's right in the middle, so look closely."

The astronauts leaned in to see if they could detect some other image on the black and white photograph. There it was; a drawing of a square with a straight horizontal line floating underneath.

"So what does that mean?" Adam asked with a perplexed look.

Chris answered him after a long delay.

"We don't know. Our guys are stumped. We've got a team of mathematicians trying to decipher it. Whatever it is, I hope it's wonderful. *And friendly.*"

"Thanks. I guess we'll find out soon," Adam replied.

CHAPTER 15

When done correctly, space travel can be quite boring. The remaining portion of the voyage passed without any major stumbling blocks. The astronauts went through their checklists. They ate. They slept. They talked. They didn't die. They didn't kill each other. The big blue ball got smaller and the little red dot got bigger.

The Little Turtle was no longer hurtling through the vast emptiness of space. Right now the only sound on board was that of the various computer cooling fans. Several days earlier, the MM10 motors had been turned around to help slow it down, eventually using the outer Martian atmosphere for auxiliary braking purposes.

Each of the four explorers commandeered one of the porthole windows. They stared out at the giant red sphere floating in front of them. After nearly twenty eight days, they were now in a stable orbit around the Red Planet and would stay there until the landing sequence was initiated.

For the first time since they left the International Space Station, the astronauts were once again floating inside the cabin. It took some getting used to. Adam and Keller goofed around with the weightlessness by doing body flips. Loud static sounds suddenly emanated from the speakers, followed by the sound of talking.

"Little Turtle, this is Mission Control. Do you read me?"

The crackly voice was barely intelligible over the intercom.

Adam broke away from the floating fun and wandered over to the communications panel. He turned on the microphone and adjusted some of the knobs.

"We hear you loud and clear. We've achieved a stable orbit around Mars. We plan to start the landing sequence in thirty minutes. Please advise."

It would take nearly five minutes for that message to get to Earth and just as long for NASA's reply to reach them with further instructions. This was very different from the Moon missions where the messages only took about one second to travel between the astronauts and Mission Control.

Keller was floating in front of the large porthole window. "I can't stop staring at it. The giant red orb. It's just, big... and rusty."

"I hear you," Adam replied. "And just think. We'll be walking around on it very soon."

Keller looked at Adam to say something, but he stopped and turned back to stare out the window, afraid he would miss something.

Adam and Yeva floated up to the flight deck. He pulled out two green three-ring binders and gave one to Yeva. They began to go through several checklists; if all went well, they could consider initiating the descent process. Once it was started, they could not stop. In a very short time, they would either be on the surface of Mars or *in the surface* of Mars.

Adam had forgotten about Mission Control already. Suddenly, he was startled when the reply arrived after it's long transit from Earth.

"Congratulations crew. Everybody is going crazy down here with tension. All systems look good. Proceed with the landing sequence at your discretion."

"Roger that, Mission Control," Adam replied. "We'll send you a message once we land. Little Turtle, out."

The astronauts made their way to their closets and put on their space suits and helmets. They floated back to the flight deck and strapped themselves into their seats in preparation for landing.

"Just think, we're about to land on a planet that is completely inhabited by robots," Adam joked, attempting to cut through the tension.

The crew snickered.

Adam closely watched a display on the computer screen that showed their approximate position over the surface of Mars. It consisted of some satellite imagery overlaid with a grid. Once the ship passed over a mountain named Aeolis Mons (Mount Sharp), he would start the descent sequence. This would put them down at right about where the housing unit had landed, not far from the fossils.

He stared intently at the screen and waited. Over the horizon came an enormous mountain. It passed under his target site. He lifted the protected toggle switch cover and pressed two red buttons. The Little Turtle jerked, and a few mechanical *clunks* were heard. Those were the traditional rocket-engine landing systems coming alive and filling with fuel. The astronauts felt a slight deceleration as the small retro rockets fired off and on for a period of a few seconds. After a few cycles, the engines turned off and stayed off.

Adam looked at the others and said, "That's it. We slowed down enough for gravity to start pulling us in. Once we get low enough, we'll fire the main descent rockets full blast and navigate our way to the Big Turtle."

The descent started out very smooth. The atmosphere was so thin they didn't experience the same type of buffeting that the space shuttle experiences when returning to Earth. After a few minutes, the ship started to creak and moan. Aerodynamic stresses on the structure were causing the metal bulkheads to oilcan, making popping sounds. The noise made Adam nervous.

Please stop the noise, please stop the noise, he thought to himself.

Molly monitored the life support systems.

"All support systems are good!"

The astronauts no longer saw the edge of the planet. It was all red from their view, with streaks of dark brown and some black. The ship was descending into the Martian afternoon haze.

The occasional shake turned into a constant vibration. The noises got louder by the second.

"Our altitude is about 2200 meters!" Adam yelled.

The other astronauts looked at each other. The shaking was getting more violent than they had expected. Adam stared at the screen intently; something wasn't right.

"We're falling too fast!" Adam blurted out. "Our descent

rockets won't be able to stop us."

Keller's eyes were wide open now, and his heart pounded. He would be the first rich man to die on Mars. He assumed they would name the impact crater after him.

Adam had a hard time focusing on the computer screen due to the shaking.

"We're going too fast! I'm gonna to have to use our return parachutes!" he yelled.

"But those are for the landing back on *Earth*," Yeva yelled at him. "If you use them now, we'll be doomed!"

"And if I don't, we'll be dead!" Adam screamed.

He reached up to a panel on the top and grabbed a big red handle marked *Parachute Override*. He yanked down on it. Nothing happened. He tried again and his hand slid off the handle. He grabbed it again and yanked. Nothing.

The ship bucked violently. He grabbed the handle with both hands and pulled so hard he lifted himself against his seatbelt straps. *Clunk!* Three long ropes deployed from the roof of the Little Turtle. At the end of the ropes, three enormous parachutes exploded open and filled with the thin Martian air. The vehicle slowed down so quickly that the astronauts' heads slammed backwards.

The buffeting stopped. The rattle stopped. Keller's heart stopped (*or so he thought*). Adam started breathing again.

They dangled beneath the three giant parachutes, but nowhere near the surface housing unit.

"Okay, we're at about 400 meters," Adam declared. "I'll be using the descent rockets to lower us down and guide us. We're still hanging from parachutes, but the rockets are going to do the steering."

He flipped two red switches on the panel and grabbed

the joystick which controlled the rocket vectoring. His eyes squinted while he tried to watch several charts on the computer screen simultaneously along with instruments on the control panel. Adam carefully guided the ship as it descended under the restraint of the parachutes.

Yeva looked out the window and saw the housing unit.

"There's the Big Turtle! Keep going forward. We're not far now."

"I see it on the navigation screen. We're almost there," Adam said.

He throttled up the engines as they got closer to the ground — the rumble echoed throughout the interior of Little Turtle. The engines kicked up the red Martian sand, gravel and dust. A huge cloud of dust was now obscuring the windows.

"We're at ten meters. Eight meters. Hang on... okay, four meters. Here we go, folks."

Clunk.

For the first time in a month, they were on something very solid — they could feel it in their stomachs. The sound of the parachutes falling on top of the Little Turtle was loud; like ropes falling on the roof of a school bus. Adam turned off the engines. All was quiet except for the sound of their own heartbeats.

Adam had never been so relieved. He picked up the microphone.

"Mission Control, the Little Turtle has landed successfully on the surface of Mars. I repeat, Little Turtle has landed. No system faults are being reported as of right now."

Adam stared at the blinking red light that signified the parachutes had been used prematurely. No need to explain that part of the descent to Mission Control just yet. They would figure it out. It was time to breathe now.

"Well, we didn't die," Adam said. "I'm glad that's over."

The gravity of what they'd just accomplished matched the gravity holding them in their seats. They grinned from ear to ear. The crew knew that even if they went no further, they had just changed human history. They alone had just advanced our species to another planet.

In a little over ten minutes, the astronauts would hear back from Earth.

CHAPTER 16

"Why is there so much static coming from the speakers?" Keller asked with a confused look on his face.

Once they were on the surface, their communication with Earth relied on an intermediary satellite in orbit around Mars named *Odyssey*. It had been sent there years earlier, mainly to measure thermal surface data. If that satellite failed, they would only have a direct line of communication with Earth for a few hours every day. Adam was now concerned that the relay satellite was malfunctioning.

Yeva's frown turned to a grin. She laughed.

"I think that *static* is the sound of cheering from Mission Control."

She was right. The sound of a hundred people clapping and yelling overwhelmed the microphones at Mission Control. Eventually, the crew could distinguish a voice talking over the cheers. It was the Mission Control Director speaking to them.

"Okay guys, we can finally breathe!" the Mission Control director said over the speakers. "The entire room — no, the entire *planet* is going nuts down here. There is confetti falling in Times Square!"

"They like us. I think they really, *really* like us," Keller joked.

Mission Control continued talking, "Hey guys, somebody here has a few words for you."

Adam raised his hand. "Be quiet everybody."

"To the group of men and women who just took our species from this planet to the next, you have my wholehearted thanks for taking on this audacious task and making it happen. Godspeed to your exploration, experiments, and a safe trip home."

And that was it. The culmination of mankind's hard work wrapped up in a few words from the president of the United States of America. His re-election was now guaranteed.

Mission Control started talking again.

"Thank you, President Jennings. We have another message. This one is for *Yeva*."

For the next minute, the Russian president spoke directly to Yeva in her native language. None of the other crew could understand it. When she smiled and her eyes filled with tears, Adam realized it was something heartfelt.

Mission Control knew the astronauts had a big job to do and decided to keep this talk short.

"Those were some special words from the world leaders responsible for this mission. Crew, we're going to sign off now, but we'll be calling again soon. Mission Control, out."

Adam was the first out of his seat, happy to walk with solid gravity again. He weighed a little over a third of what he did on Earth, but the constant gravity felt good and reassuring. He tried a little hop, but banged his head on the low ceiling.

"Congratulations, everybody," he said in a fatherly tone. "From now on, every step you take is history in the making."

As much as they wanted to get outside and walk around, their first task was to make sure the life support systems were working. After that, they had to extend the pressurized hallway from the Little Turtle all the way to the Big Turtle, which had arrived a few weeks earlier.

The Little Turtle sat on four landing pads; each pad had powered wheels on the bottom. The entire vehicle automatically crawled slowly toward the Big Turtle until the pressurized hallway was near the hatch on the other side of the gap. Once everything was aligned, the hallway would extend, crossing the chasm between the two modules. The result would be an air-filled walkway between them. When the connection was made, it would virtually triple the available living space. That was the plan.

Adam paused the hallway extension unexpectedly.

"Hang on, everybody. We can't extend the hallway until we drop the grounding cables. Otherwise, we'll have all kinds of nasty static electricity problems when the hallway touches the other ship."

Adam lifted a small panel near the hallway hatch and exposed two red switches. He pushed the first switch down. Underneath the Little Turtle, a spike fired downward from an air cannon at high speed. It drove deep into the bedrock and dragged a steel woven cable with it. Adam flipped the other switch and a similar spike fired from the bottom of the Big Turtle. Both ships were now electrically grounded. Any static electricity buildup from the constant blowing winds would be dissipated easily through the cables and into the ground beneath.

Adam returned his attention to making the extendable hallway cross the gap over to the Big Turtle. The astronauts watched out the windows as this delicate mechanical dance took place. The control computer took the lead to this waltz automatically.

The hallway support wheels slowly rolled along the Martian surface, leaving a rut in the loose soil. When it reached about half way, one of its support wheels ran into a rock on the ground that was just taller than it could climb. Normally, it would back off and try to roll around the obstacle. This was a wide rock though, and it was a serious problem.

"Crap, we didn't plan on that," Adam said, frowning with irritation. "We have to get that hallway attached, or the mission just got more complicated — the airlock for external excursions is on the *Big Turtle*. We can't exit Little Turtle without depressurizing the entire ship. We could do that, but I'd rather not."

"We need to push that rock out of the way, right?" Yeva asked. "Sounds like the perfect task for our mini-rover, yes?"

"Yeva, you are brilliant," Adam replied, smiling.

He walked over to the rover station and lifted the handheld control transmitter out of the wall caddy. Although the mini-rover was meant for surface exploration purposes, nobody said it couldn't be used for a little rock bulldozing.

Adam held what looked just like any common radio-controlled toy transmitter. He pushed a button labeled *Extend*. A noisy ramp extended from the bottom of the ship until it pushed into the red dust beneath the ship. The rover itself resembled a small toy Jeep about three feet long. It rolled down the ramp and onto the ground. Adam pushed the throttle stick frontwards, and the mini-rover took off like a rocket.

"Whoa! That little thing is fast!" Adam yelled.

"Slow down there, cheetah," Keller said, laughing.

Adam used smaller stick movements and brought it back around, maneuvering it next to the problem rock. He used the mini-rover's claw attachment to grab the rock and roll it out of the way. As he did that, the hallway extension jerked back into motion and continued moving toward Big Turtle.

"Aren't you glad they kept that mini-rover in the budget?" Yeva smiled.

Adam looked relieved.

After a few more minutes of motion, a loud *clunk* was heard and the ship shook. They looked out the windows and saw that the hallway was now attached to Big Turtle, forming a bridge to their new living quarters. It was pressurizing and would be viable in a short while.

Adam wanted to remove his helmet, but he knew that would be unsafe until they established that the hallway was now an airtight connection between two airtight ships. He opened the door on Little Turtle giving him access to the newly extended hallway. The sound of rushing air lasted just a few seconds. Everything seemed okay.

There were no surprises in sight or sound. He walked

carefully to the other end of the hallway, each step causing it to bounce up and down like a cheaply built bridge. Adam found himself standing just outside the door on Big Turtle.

He grabbed hold of the circular handle on the door and slowly spun it. It opened. He felt a blast of air hit his suit, pushing him backwards. He instinctively held his breath, even though he was still wearing his helmet. Had he not been holding onto the door handle, the push of air would have knocked him down. The rush of air was a good sign — it meant that Big Turtle was pressurized.

Adam pushed hard on the door and peered in through the opening. He pushed it wide open and looked around, checking a pressure gauge on the wall. He turned around and looked back through the hallway at the other astronauts. They anxiously awaited his next step. His hands came up, he took off his helmet, slowly at first and finally with a quick movement.

"We're home, kids. Take off your helmets and stay a while!"

The next hour was a flurry of activity. Each astronaut got out their purple checklists and went through them meticulously. Adam was to check all of the safety systems and valves. Molly made sure the life support systems were functioning and that they had enough oxygen to supply their 30 day mission. Yeva was opening all of the exploration tool compartments to check their condition.

Keller, on the other hand, was staring out the window at the red rocky landscape just a few feet away. To him, it looked like Arizona. Being on such a huge planet with only a confined place to survive caused his hands to begin shaking.

When nobody was looking, Keller took one of his pills. He calmed down.

Yeva had the delicate task of dropping the Mars small space exploration vehicle, or sSEV, from the Big Turtle housing module. The astronauts referred to it as the *golf cart*. Although NASA had developed surface exploration vehicles for future missions, the sSEV was a quickly-developed smaller version to fit this mission. It literally looked like an open-air golf cart with big wheels and solar panels on top. It had to be slid out on extendable rods where it would drop onto the surface. This golf cart is what the astronauts would use to drive around during their external excursions. It was their main vehicle.

Yeva sat down at the control panel by the airlock. This gave her a good view outside. She could see the golf cart pinned against the side of Big Turtle. She pushed the toggle switch labeled *Extend*; two large rods extended from the side of the ship carrying the golf cart with it. Next she pushed the button which would release the golf cart. The rods bent down and the cart slid off. It dropped to the ground and bounced a few times. Fortunately, they couldn't hear the banging and clanging due to the thin atmosphere.

As everybody worked, they began to notice a silence that had befallen them. Nobody was talking. They just did their tasks while occasionally stealing a glance at the incredible red landscape outside their windows.

"Okay, everybody," Adam said, breaking the silence. "Let's gather around for a meeting."

The astronauts walked over to the dinner table which was rigidly bolted to the floor. They still wore the lower portion of their pressure suits.

"Once we finish these tasks," Adam explained, "I think we'll be in a good spot to start the first phase of our exploration. Yeva and I will go out first. If the golf cart is working okay, we'll drive around to examine the condition of the two Turtles from the outside. After that, we'll go find the Curiosity rover and take a look at the fossils and the pyramid. Sound good? Great."

Just prior to leaving Earth, the astronauts had secretly decided who would be the first to step down on Mars. To help choose, they had taken a bowl of pennies and each astronaut chose one. The penny with the oldest year determined who would go into the history books as being the first to walk on Mars. Yeva and Adam both picked pennies minted in 1973, the oldest pennies chosen. Never before had two cents been more valuable. After some discussion, they decided both would descend the ramp together at the same time. A coed landing of sorts. Nobody was happy with this compromise.

"It's a *green-eyed conspiracy*," Keller would later complain, referring to the fact that the two astronauts with green eyes, Adam and Yeva, would be the first people to walk on Mars. Keller and Molly were not happy about the arrangement at all, but neither complained about it during the entire voyage. They were on Mars now and they couldn't change plans. Most importantly, the arrangement was a closely held secret. Nobody outside of these four astronauts knew who would be first.

Adam wanted to be the one in the history books, though. Partly out of a sense of pride, but mainly because it would guarantee a constant stream of speaking engagements and endorsements for the rest of his life.

While moving supplies around the ship, Keller pulled Adam aside to see if he could convince him to trade places. Keller wanted that initial step on Martian soil. He looked over his shoulders to see if he could talk to Adam in privacy.

"Look, Adam," he whispered. "I have an offer for you."

"Oh yeah? I'm listening," Adam responded half-seriously while transferring a stack of supplies from one cabinet to another.

"I will pay you two million dollars if you allow me to walk out there in your place. Let me go out there with Yeva."

Adam looked at the floor, soaking in the offer.

"That's a tempting offer, Keller. *Really*. However, I think the potential payoff from being the first would far outweigh two million dollars. Besides, we may not even make it back. Then your money would be worthless to me."

"What about your family?"

Adam halted what he was working on.

"My family already has the million dollar bonus. Thanks to you, right?"

"Well, what *would* it take?" Keller asked.

"I'm afraid there's nothing you could offer. Sorry, Keller."

Keller rolled his eyes and turned away in disgust.

After the astronauts completed their task lists, Adam and Yeva prepared for their monumental trip. They put on their suits and tested the valves to make sure the pressurization was working properly. The four astronauts walked toward the airlock vestibule.

Adam and Yeva ducked through the airlock door and stood in the cramped room, staring at the external hatch. On the other side of that flimsy metal was the harsh atmosphere of Mars, with temperatures sometimes reaching minus 100 degrees Fahrenheit. Molly closed the door behind them, essentially locking in their fate. They could feel their hearts pounding.

Adam leaned toward the door and slowly rotated the handle. They heard the sound of air leaking, but it only lasted for a few seconds. Adam and Yeva stepped proudly out onto the catwalk. Stretched in front of them was a surreal landscape like no other. The common description of it looking like Arizona is not correct. It's as if a huge landscape of bedrock was sprinkled with red sand, dust and loose rocks. On Earth, even the harshest desert shows some sign of life. They could see for miles in every direction here, and there wasn't a single living organism. This place had been dead for a long time.

"It's so beautiful and so lifeless," Adam declared.

He turned his head and looked up at the roof-mounted video camera. It was beaming their images back to Earth. He waved. Billions of people were watching.

They both stood there looking down at the Martian soil. It was only three feet below them at the bottom of the ramp. It looked so inviting. History was so close. Adam's usually complacent ego was going into overdrive. He ruminated about sharing the spotlight of history. Adam's repressed arrogance flared. He had no choice.

Yeva turned her head just in time to see Adam leap forward past the end of the ramp and land on the ground. His boots kicked up a puff of dust. It blew away in the thin Martian breeze.

The ground was as solid as if he'd landed on Earth. He

stood up, soaking in an ocean of pride. In that brief betrayal of Yeva, he became the first human to step foot on another planet, ensuring his historical legacy. In five minutes, billions of people would see him become a legend.

Adam turned around and looked at Yeva. She stared at him with a look of crushing disappointment. She would always be known as the second person on Mars. In other words, she would be *unknown*. She assumed he had always planned this move.

Yeva's look of disappointment changed to rage. She reverted to her Russian and said, "Vy nakhodites' na vershine moyego spiska kormy!"

Adam raised one eyebrow. "That didn't sound like an endearing phrase."

Adam could take her derision — for now at least. Only his crew knew what was *supposed* to have happened, so he was still a hero to Mission Control and to the billions of people watching.

He pushed the glove-mounted button that opened his microphone up to the Earth video stream feed. He looked up at the camera and said what Neil Armstrong had meant to say all those years ago when he first set foot on the Moon, but Adam added a bit of political correctness too.

"This is one small step for *a human* and one giant leap for *human*kind."

Adam's name would be an answer on game shows. It would be an answer in *Trivial Pursuit: Mars Edition*. From this moment on, his family would never want for money or medicine. And all he had to do was violate a promise he had carried for many millions of miles.

Adam looked over at Yeva again.

"I'm sorry Yeva. I had to do that for my family. It's hard to explain."

Yeva was still stunned, unmoving. She walked down the ramp and stopped before reaching the dirt. She lifted her boot carefully and set it down firmly on the red dust. When she set the other boot down, she looked up at Adam.

"You can rot for all I care," she said. "Now, let us go finish what we came here for."

They walked toward the golf cart. Yeva pushed Adam out of the way as she hopped into the driver's seat.

"I am driving," she demanded.

Adam climbed onto the passenger seat.

They both reached behind their seats and pulled out an American and Russian flag respectively. They leaned out of the golf cart and jabbed them into the sandy red soil.

Adam started laughing.

"Now what could possibly be funny?" Yeva asked.

"Did you ever notice that the first two people to walk on Mars are named *Adam* and *Yeva*?" Adam asked.

She stared at him motionless.

"You know, like *Adam* and *Eve* in the Garden of Eden?"

Yeva looked at him incredulously.

He quickly added, "Granted, this place is hostile and deadly, so it's not *really* like the Garden of Eden, but still, it's a funny coincidence, right?"

Yeva was thinking. She finally spoke.

"I would like to remove one of your ribs and beat some sense into you with it."

A profound silence emerged. The smile left Adam's face.

"Okay, um..., let's get moving I guess," he said.

Yeva powered up the cart and drove a slow circle

around the Big and Little Turtles to inspect their condition. Everything looked good except for the parachutes that were lying down on the ground. Yeva pointed at them and looked at Adam for his input.

"I don't want to waste time re-packing those chutes right now. Let's continue," he commanded.

Satisfied that nothing else seemed out of place, she floored the pedal and they tore off toward the direction of the dead Curiosity rover and the fossils.

For several minutes, they wound their way around rocks, boulders and old dry river beds. The ground color alternated between dark red, light red, and the occasional black. As they crested a rocky hill, they could see what they came for.

Down in a shallow valley of smooth soil, they saw the idled Curiosity rover next to large sparkling boulders.

"That's what we came all this way to see," Adam said with a voice of amazement.

"Yes," Yeva said. "Those rocks look just like the ones in our photographs. I am excited to study the fossils up close."

It was strangely odd to see the rocks from this angle — like seeing a childhood home years after moving away. The arrangement was familiar, but the surrounding details were foreign. Behind both the rover and the fossil rock was a pyramidal structure that appeared to be made out of large flat granite walls.

"The pyramid certainly looks manmade," Yeva speculated.

"You mean *Martian* made?" Adam asked.

Yeva laughed, but quickly remembered how Adam had betrayed her. She scowled at him.

Yeva maneuvered the golf cart down the hill and parked just a few feet from the Curiosity rover. They hopped out.

Adam went to the back of the golf cart and grabbed the replacement RTG power unit and some tools. He moved them over to the Curiosity and started the laborious process of replacing its dead power unit. Adam had to work carefully because the suit gloves, although advanced, were still clunky. The RTG was wrapped in a special shroud to protect the crew from radiation. Adam focused very intently on this task.

Yeva walked over to the fossil rock and knelt down to look at it. Her knees sank into the small sand dune that had grown near the base of the boulder. She touched her glove to the bony hand fossil protruding from the stone. The hand was similar in size and shape to her own, but it was millions of years older. She was now the closest a human had ever been to an alien life form. She sat there, unmoving, as she daydreamed. Yeva imagined this place as a once luscious life-supporting landscape. She ran her fingers over the symbols on the granite block as it lay in the skeleton fossil's hand. The bony structures were embedded just in the surface of the huge rock. She took picture after picture of this most alien find.

Adam finished replacing the power unit. "There you go, *little buddy*," he said. His term of endearment was laughable, given that the Mars Curiosity Rover would weigh almost a ton on Earth. "Wander off and find some more amazing stuff."

In an hour or so, the NASA rover control center in Pasadena would direct the Curiosity to continue exploring. It would be gone from view by tomorrow morning.

As Adam walked back to the golf cart, he picked up

interesting rock samples and put them in collection bags. Most were rust colored, but a few had greenish tint and sparkly quartz. If they had to abort the mission for any reason, at least they'd have these priceless treasures to take back to Earth.

Adam put his tools and collection bags back in the golf cart. He picked up his digital camera and started taking high-resolution photos of the fossils near Yeva.

"I gotta admit," he said. "They look posed. Almost like they were put here on purpose to *become* fossils."

"Possibly, but how do you think they went about embedding them in rock like this? I hope the person was already dead when they put them here so long ago."

Adam examined the boulder closely.

"I don't think this boulder is a naturally occurring rock formation. It looks more like concrete to me. Except, instead of using gravel, they used greenish gems. Maybe *olivine*? Why would they do that?" Adam asked.

"My guess is they wanted to grab the attention of any future travelers. It sure got *our* attention, yes?" Yeva wondered.

"Good point," Adam replied.

The only visible parts on the fossils were the hands, arms, and legs. The head was partially visible, but mostly encased in the gem-infused boulder. Upon closer inspection, the symbols in the granite block were inlaid in gold.

"In hindsight," Adam stated, "it seems obvious now that these lines represent Pi. Just like *Chris* said."

Yeva was the only crewmember who had guessed that correctly. She ignored Adam's statement.

"Look at those leg bone fragments," she pointed. "This

person was extremely tall. I suspect seven, maybe eight feet tall? Must be the result of living with lower gravity."

"That's not the only strange thing here," Adam said. "Have you noticed how this symbol stone and the pyramid are the only examples of granite within sight? Just look around. All I see are random volcanic stones and some broken sedimentary rocks. There's some basalt over there. I wonder where they got the granite from?"

Yeva nodded her head in agreement.

"There must be a quarry somewhere around here. The ground cover is interesting, too. It looks like sand mixed with red dust. I move my hand through it, and it's just so light, yet on top of a very hard crust. It's like we're only inches from bedrock."

Over the radio came a transmission from Keller.

"Hey, have you guys found anything yet? Your little jumping stunt has reached Earth and returned. The crowds are going wild."

Adam laughed and said, "Yeah, I'm not sure what came over me; I must've lost my footing or something."

Yeva stared at him with hateful eyes.

"We're at the site," Adam continued. "I replaced the power unit on the Curiosity, and we're looking at the fossils now. The symbols are much more impressive in person. Isn't that right, Yeva?"

He looked up to see her still staring at him with disdain.

Yeva hoped he would fall down and break his legs. She would pose his skeleton next to the fossils for the next civilization to find.

"Now, don't go stealing those artifacts. Me and Molly want to see them too," Keller said.

Yeva brought out her toolkit and took a few samples of the fossils from the boulder. She put them in plastic bags to be examined later.

After taking some more pictures, Adam noted that they had already burned through half of their oxygen — the fuel cells that were utilized to heat their suits were using a bit more oxygen than NASA had predicted.

The two astronauts walked over toward the pyramid structure. On the side facing them was a big round disk made of smooth rock, leaning against the pyramid. In the middle of the door was an engraved square shown floating over a straight line. Additionally, there was also a ring of symbols going around the outer edge of the door. This detail hadn't been visible in the photographs. These etchings were much more elaborate than those in the fossil's hand.

"It looks like the sign on the door has an added bonus for us," Adam remarked. "Wish I knew what it meant."

Yeva used her fossil brush to clean the dust out of each engraving. She documented all of them quickly with her camera. While she worked, Adam walked around the outside perimeter of the building to see if there were any other potential entrances. When he arrived back, Yeva asked, "See any other openings?"

"No," Adam answered. "Nothing else."

"Well, do you think the door rolls open or maybe it swings on hinges?" Yeva asked.

"I doubt metal door hinges would've lasted long, so they probably used the classic rolling slab door. Whatever it is, I sure hope it's hiding something awesome inside."

"How should we move it?" Yeva wondered.

The two explorers looked around for some clues about

how to roll this big round door away. Adam pushed on it hard. It didn't budge. He returned to the golf cart. He pulled the utility shovel from it and brought it back to the round door.

"Maybe if I dig away the sand from one side of the door, it'll roll away?"

He started digging, taking big scoops of the red sand and tossing it aside.

Suddenly, the ground shook. It shook a lot. Adam stopped digging. He saw the golf cart rocking back and forth, too. The shimmying lasted for five seconds before fading. Sand shifted away from the circular door.

Adam asked over the headset microphone, "Hey, did anybody else feel that Earthquake?"

"You mean *Marsquake*?" Keller replied over the intercom.

"Yeah, I suppose that's what I meant. It's stopped now."

"Yes, we felt some shaking, but it didn't last long," Keller said.

Adam was flustered, but he continued removing sand from one side of the circular door.

After a few minutes, the round door began to roll toward the low point, albeit slowly. Adam tried to push it again, but it didn't budge. He took a break and gave the shovel to Yeva. After digging some more, the disc rolled far enough to the side for the two astronauts to squeeze by, but only if they turned sideways.

"Hey, Yeva. How much oxygen do you have?" Adam asked.

Yeva looked at the gauge on her wrist.

"About 15 minutes. We'll have time to go in and take a

few pictures."

"Okay. This is it, everybody," Adam announced over the intercom. "We are now going to enter a room built by aliens. Can you believe it?"

"Go for it," Molly responded.

Adam walked back to the golf cart to grab the tripod-mounted floodlight. He planned to use it to illuminate the interior of the pyramid. Adam hefted it up and laid it against his shoulder. When he turned around, Yeva was gone.

CHAPTER 17

"Yeva! Yeva! Where are you? Yevaaa!" Adam yelled into his headset microphone. He spun around frantically looking for her. His eyes searched the ground for bootprints.

"Relax, mutton-head," the voice of Yeva crackled in his headset. "I am inside the pyramid. I wanted to be the first at *something.*"

"We gotta work as a team and not lose each other," Adam said excitedly. "Just like in training — we have to use the buddy system."

"Seriously? Okay, we will work as a team from now on," she replied with thick sarcasm.

Adam could see her flashlight beam moving around, just inside the doorway. He jogged over to the opening and peeked into the darkness. His right hand reached up to his helmet and flipped two switches. The first engaged a helmet-mounted flashlight. The second turned on the helmet-mounted video camera — it would record all the amazing things they were about to see.

Adam turned sideways and squeezed through the door opening. *Think thin*, he thought. Once through, he walked over to the middle of the room. His flashlight sent an erratic beam all over the floor.

Adam set the floodlight down on the ground and spread out the tripod legs one by one. This was no normal floodlight. It contained a large omnidirectional LED bulb that was brighter than most normal floodlights back on Earth. He reached just beneath the bulb and turned on the power switch. The entire room lit up like Texas at lunchtime. The two explorers immediately realized that the building was split into two rooms — a vertical stone wall partially separated the spaces. The room they were standing in was much larger than the other room. With limited oxygen, they decided to focus on the room they were in.

Gray granite walls surrounded them; polished flat and filled with meticulously engraved carvings. This was not caveman art. With all of the sharp angles and elaborate curves, this was the work of intelligent beings.

Adam and Yeva both found themselves drawn toward the walls. They wanted to experience the feel of the precisely cut characters. The indentations were large enough for their gloves to follow them.

"If I didn't know any better," Adam pondered out loud, "I'd say this is an advanced written language. Discrete characters made with only a few strokes and the occasional dot. Looks closer to English than, say, Chinese. What do you think Yeva?"

"It is so beautiful. Not sure what to make of it. It actually looks a lot like proto-Elamite. In style at least."

"Yes, yes," Adam agreed. "And *what* is proto-Elamite?"

Yeva turned and looked at him incredulously. "And you call yourself a scientist?"

"No, I'm half-engineer and half-geologist. That makes me an *engeologist*," Adam joked.

"And a complete traitor," she accused, looking back at the glyphs. "Proto-Elamite is the oldest undeciphered written language on Earth."

"Wow," Adam exclaimed, raising his eyebrows. "That is something."

Yeva rubbed her gloves on the smooth granite, "How has the granite not lost its polish after millions of years?"

Adam and Yeva walked along the walls, recording as much as they could on their helmet-mounted video cameras. Simultaneously, each of them took high-resolution photographs with hand-held digital SLR cameras that had been modified to work in the Mars atmosphere. Eventually, they found themselves standing next to a granite block near the back of the room. The block was roughly the size of a dinner table. Adam stared at it in confusion.

"And then there's *that* thing," he said sarcastically.

On the four exposed sides were groupings of letters. Words perhaps, organized into paragraphs. On the large top surface was a string of characters all evenly spaced with large gaps in between each one.

"These carvings on the top must be their alphabet. Each letter is so delicately drawn," Adam pondered with amazement.

Under each letter was a column that contained tightly packed horizontal grooves, like the cross-section of an old vinyl album with tiny hills and valleys.

Yeva was photographing all of these while Adam, in a

trance, slid his finger along each of the engraved letters and counted them.

As he traced each letter, he realized that he was the first sentient being to do this in millions of years. *The person who carved these must've done the same thing with his fingers,* Adam thought.

"Twenty-nine letters. Amazing, eh? Millions of years and millions of miles apart, and yet, our alphabets are so close in size."

Yeva motioned for him to move his hand away so she could take more pictures.

"Hey Yeva, what do you think of all the writing on the side of this block?"

Yeva paused to think about Adam's question. She nodded her head and answered, "It appears to be some type of Rosetta stone, perhaps. You know, the same story told on all four sides, but each side in a different language to help some future translator. Unfortunately, we now see the same story in four languages that we can't read."

A slow beep started. Adam looked down at his oxygen gauge.

"Uh oh. Ten minute warning — gotta get going. We'll leave the floodlight here. Did you get a lot of photos?" Adam asked as he walked over and turned off the floodlight.

Yeva nodded her confirmation. "Yes. Lots of pictures. When we get back to the Big Turtle, we can upload them to the NASA servers. Maybe the NSA guys can work their magic on this alphabet."

The two astronauts walked toward the dusty sunbeam shining through the thin door opening. They squeezed through the gap and trudged over the red sand toward the golf cart. Yeva once again hopped into the driver's seat before Adam had a chance. He climbed into the other seat. She pressed the accelerator pedal and they took off up the hill, sending a rooster tail of cloudy scarlet dust.

"Hey, Molly. Hey, Keller. Do you hear me?" Adam asked over the main headset communication link.

"Yup, loud and clear," Keller replied.

"Well, Mom and Dad are on their way back. Hope we won't be interrupting you two," Adam said as he grinned and winked at Yeva. She did not smile.

Keller sat with his boots up on the main table. He saw a red cloud of dust in the distance. The cloud seemed to eject a slow moving golf cart. He casually wandered over to the airlock control panel, ready to let the weary travelers back into the life boat.

Keller hummed the lyrics to his favorite space song: *"Rocket maaaan, burning down the trees on every lawn..."*

The cart pulled up next to the ramp, but Yeva backed it up into the direct sunlight. She hopped out and gathered up the cameras and fossil samples. Adam deployed the solar array to charge the batteries on the golf cart.

The two explorers made their way up the ramp and into the airlock. Keller pushed a sequence of switches which flooded the evacuated vestibule with breathable oxygen. Simultaneously, a strong fan in the ceiling of the airlock blew a powerful wind over them. It removed any Martian dust that may have collected on their suits. Finally, the door opened. Yeva walked in first and removed her helmet. Keller welcomed her back, shaking her hand.

"Did you see any little green men?" he asked.

"No," Yeva quickly answered, "but did you see what this arrogant monster did to me during our walk down to the surface?"

Keller felt like he was stuck in the middle of a messy domestic quarrel.

"Um, yeah," he said. "We noticed that. Fortunately, nobody at Mission Control knew what was supposed to happen. And may I congratulate *you*, Yeva, for not punching Adam on live television in front of billions of people."

Adam redirected the mood. "We did take a lot of photos. Let's get them uploaded to NASA, pronto."

"We have some samples from the fossils, too," Yeva added. "Let's get them into the thermal ionization spectrometer right away and find out exactly how old they are."

Molly hooked up the cameras to her laptop. After some fiddling with the software, she started the upload process. This would move gigabytes of photograph files through the long void of space to the high-bandwidth antenna on the International Space Station, before finally going to the NASA servers at the Mission Control Center in Houston. This process took over two hours. The combination of large files, large distances, and error correction algorithms complicated the transfer. When it was all done, they had a teleconference with Chris Tankovitch to discuss what they'd found.

"Thank you everybody," Chris said, excitedly as he viewed the images on a nearby monitor. "The media is itching to get ahold of these."

The ten minute round-trip delay made communication very difficult. At the end of the disjointed discussion, Chris congratulated them and made some assurances.

"We have top mathematicians and paleographers here in this building, trying to decipher this language as we speak. If they can't do it, we have some backup ideas. Wish us luck."

After ending the teleconference with Chris, they started the night-time process of shutting things down. The astronauts had been awake for a long time now and could barely keep their eyes open as they climbed into their bunks.

"I have a feeling we'll find something amazing in that other room tomorrow," Adam admitted to the group.

"Hopefully. *Good night*," Molly said.

"Good night," Yeva said.

"Good night, John-Boy. Good night girls," Keller laughed.

The Sun set and pitch-black darkness took over the cabin interior. They fell asleep quickly and easily for the first time in over a month.

CHAPTER 18

"Rise and shine, slumber-heads," Adam announced as the automated window blinds rolled up. "I've got hot liquefied waffles and milk for everybody."

Rays of morning sunshine cascaded through the Big Turtle's interior. One by one, the other crewmembers pried open their eyes to see breakfast set out on the main table.

"Yummo," Keller said.

The astronauts gathered around the table and ate their boxes of goo and drank their bags of milk, water and coffee.

"Have either of you thought more about what you saw in the pyramid?" Molly asked.

Adam nodded. "I still don't have a clue what those engravings meant, but I'm sure it was an alphabet. Very similar to the pronto-Laminate language."

"I'm sure you mean *proto-Elamite*," Molly said, giggling.

"Yes, that is what I taught him yesterday," Yeva

explained. "His inflated head makes him forgetful. Please pass the coffee bag."

Adam tried to redirect the conversation. "Anyhow, inside that pyramid it felt like we were surrounded by tombstones and epitaphs. I suppose they had to write in stone to preserve the information for so long."

Keller looked around the group. "Tombstones and epitaphs? On that cheery note, Dr. Life Support, do you have our oxygen tanks ready to go?"

Molly smiled and put her hand on his arm.

"Why, yes, Keller Murch. They are ready for you to use on your pyramid adventure today."

"Just so everybody knows," Adam interrupted, "the portable fuel cells in the suits are using a bit more oxygen than predicted. The excursion times will be shorter than we were planning. Just watch your gauges."

"Duly noted," Molly said.

"We'll get cleaned up and get ready to go," Adam said. "Today's job is to photograph the secondary room in the pyramid. While we're away from the Turtles, why don't you two drop the caisson and start on the soil experiments?"

The group cleaned off the table and ran through the daily checklists. Adam set up the video chat link with NASA for their first post-Mars-walk interview with the media. Only Yeva and Adam were requested for the chat.

They once again realized that a ten-plus minute round-trip delay wreaks havoc on interpersonal communication. NASA arranged for the astronauts to receive a list of questions ahead of time and would answer them nonstop in a stream. The questions ranged from the mundane (How do you pee in space?) to pretty extraordinary (What color is the sky on Mars?).

Adam completed the media conference by saying, "Okay, folks, I hope you enjoyed our little talk. I know that we did."

Adam looked over at Keller. "Are you ready to walk on an alien planet?"

"I don't know. Are you going to jump in front of me, too?" Keller asked with a smirk.

Adam stared at Keller for a long time, squinting his eyes in derision.

They put on their pressure suits and walked over to the airlock. Adam opened the door and stepped in, quickly followed by Keller. Each astronaut inspected his oxygen gauge and gave Molly the thumbs-up sign. She closed the door behind them and activated the air evacuation process. The two astronauts heard the *whoosh* of the air escaping. Adam turned the big handle on the outside door and it popped open.

Keller walked out, only to be blinded by the Mars sunrise. The sky was a mixture of colors, from pinkish red to gray. This pastel morning sky was the most beautiful thing he'd ever seen. Keller stared at the horizon, barely blinking as he consumed the panoramic landscape.

"Wow...," Keller whispered.

Adam put his glove on Keller's shoulder and said, "It's a sight to behold, isn't it? Let's go."

It was obvious to Keller that Adam didn't care much about what they were doing anymore. Adam had completed his goal of being first on Mars; now, he wanted to get home and cash in those chips. This was just a stop on the journey — an item on his to-do list.

Adam folded down the solar arrays on the golf cart and they both climbed in. Keller sat in the driver's seat.

Adam pointed toward the sunrise.

"Just follow our tracks from yesterday," he commanded.

Keller accelerated, following the tracks exactly. It was the easiest path he'd ever driven. The cart's wheels threw up a rooster tail of red dust.

"Man, this is just like driving on my beach back home."

They crested over the ridge and coasted down toward the pyramid. Keller stopped just a few feet from the big circular stone door. He stepped out of the golf cart and walked back towards the fossil boulder that started this whole adventure. He leaned down and carefully examined the fossils, being careful not to touch them. After a short time, he felt something was missing from the scene and stood up.

"Where's the Curiosity rover?" Keller asked.

"I guess it already left on another adventure," Adam said, craning his neck around to scan the site. "That replacement power unit gave it a new lease on life."

Each astronaut grabbed a handheld camera from the golf cart and crawled back into the pyramid through the small door opening. They both turned on their helmet-mounted flashlights and video cameras. Adam turned on the floodlight-tripod.— bright light illuminated the entire pyramid interior.

"Whoa!" Keller said as he drank in the ancient museum ambiance.

"I agree with that sentiment," Adam approved. "Look around. Check out all of these engravings. It's amazing stuff."

The two astronauts walked over to the walls and ran their gloved fingers through the engravings. Adam showed the table-sized granite block to Keller who quickly leaned down to examine all four sides. After Adam showed Keller all that he and Yeva had found, Adam walked over to the floodlight and picked it up.

"Let's move this light over to the other side. Follow me."

Their shadows wobbled all around as Adam carried the floodlight. They eased around the large divider wall. The style of the symbols carved into the new walls was different. These looked more mathematical in nature: lots of right-angles and circles. Adam couldn't decide if it looked more like geometry or chemistry. He set down the floodlight.

"What the heck is that?" Keller asked, pointing to a small black cube floating just a few inches above what looked like a granite pedestal.

They walked directly over to it and stared quizzically. The small black cube floated above the table surface. Keller poked it and the cube drifted across the top of the pedestal. He poked it from the opposite side to keep it from falling off.

Adam raised a skeptical eyebrow and repeated what Keller had just done, poking the cube with his finger. Once again, it started to drift across the pedestal. However, this time he didn't stop it. He let it drift. And it didn't fall down once it left the pedestal top. In fact, it just kept on gliding at the same height. Adam poked the bottom of the cube, and it started to drift upward at an angle. He stopped it before it got too high. This little cube seemed to completely ignore gravity.

Keller and Adam looked around again, noticing this time that the room seemed to be dedicated to this cube.

"You know — I can't figure it out," Adam pondered. "Is this room a gift to future explorers or some kind of shrine to this cube? I mean, this thing looks like anti-gravity, but that's not possible. If I remember my physics class, Einstein's general relativity states that anti-gravity can't exist."

Keller put his glove on Adam's shoulder. "Either you've got a crappy memory, or Albert was wrong."

With new excitement, Adam took a slew of photographs of everything on the walls. Keller continued playing with the floating cube.

"Wow, wow, wow," Adam said, pausing his picture-taking. "This could be the biggest thing to ever happen to science. I don't understand the drawings here, but they must be trying to explain how this cube works."

"I'll admit," Keller quipped. "This is probably bigger than sliced bread or the keyless chuck."

As they were photographing the peculiar cube, a crackly message from Yeva arrived over their headsets.

"..... Adam.... Kell.... We just got some news from the NSA on the language. They cracked it overnight. They sa... that it is a short hist..."

Adam and Keller looked at each other and shook their heads — neither one could understood her message.

"Yeva, we're having a hard time hearing you," Adam replied. "Hang on, we're going to walk closer to the door."

The two astronauts walked over toward the door opening. Yeva's voice became crystal clear.

"Okay, Yeva, you said they cracked the language code already? How'd they do it so fast?"

"The NSA paleographers sent the photographs out to universities around the planet. A grad student at the Moscow

State University cracked it. *My alma mater*. Go me!"

"So they crowd-sourced it?" Keller asked. "Very clever."

"They think the engravings are a history lesson of some kind, that talk about how the Martians created something and it caused their society to run out of food and water. The NSA have not deciphered what that creation was yet, but it is related to the extra signage found on the circular door. Those phrases are repeated several times."

Adam and Keller looked at each other and shrugged their shoulders.

"By the way," Yeva continued, "you will laugh, but these ancient Mars people are now being called *The Curiosities* by the media, named after the rover."

Yeva chuckled after stating the new name.

"Anyhow, the Curiosities planned to move many of their people to the third planet from the star. Obviously, we can assume they are referring to Earth. It had more land and water and could be used as a farming colony. However, that planet had some rather intelligent, yet *violent*, animals that needed to be dealt with before it could be a safe place for them to inhabit. They were also worried about the intense gravity on Earth."

"Are they referring to the *dinosaurs*?" Keller asked, very proud of himself.

Yeva paused. Adam and Keller heard the muffled sounds of Yeva talking to somebody else.

"Okay, sorry," she said. "Molly had a question that I had to answer. So these Curiosities sent a team of explorers, but never heard from them again. It says they are still waiting for their children to return. It keeps referring to the explorers as their *children*. They miss them dearly."

Adam and Keller stood silent, contemplating the sad message.

"Sounds like things didn't go well for them," Adam surmised. "Thanks, Yeva. Is that, um…, is that everything?"

"No, there is more," Yeva added. "Do you remember that Rosetta stone block with the alphabet on top and the serrated columns under each letter?"

Adam instinctively pointed his head-mounted flashlight toward the large table-sized block.

"Yes. Keller and I can see it right now."

"Well, those serrated columns are audio strips. They encoded the sound waves required to pronounce their letters. They wanted to preserve not only their written language, but also the spoken form of it. That is very arrogant, yes?"

Adam started laughing.

"Why are you laughing?" Yeva asked.

"When I was a kid," Adam explained, "they had birthday party balloons with hard plastic sticks as handles. Well, the sticks had serrated ridges on them and when you ran your finger nail down the edge, it would literally sound out messages like 'happy birthday.' They never worked right and it always sounded like 'yappee wormway.' I guess there is nothing new under the Sun."

"Maybe they just wanted to preserve as much of their culture as they could before the end came," Keller suggested. "They must've had time to see it coming. How awful."

"One more thing," Yeva interrupted. "I saved the best for last. I completed a dating analysis on those fossil bone samples. There is a problem with our original theory. They are not two million years old."

Keller smiled proudly. "See, I told you. *Dinosaurs.*

These fossils must be sixty-five million years old! Heck, these Curiosities are what killed off the dinosaurs!"

"Anyhow...," Adam said with concern, "how far off did we get the age?"

"To our surprise, they are still mostly bone. Not fossils. Our dating analysis says they are only about two hundred *thousand* years old. Not two *million*. And certainly not sixty-five million. Sorry, Keller. A meteor still killed the dinosaurs."

"Are you sure?" Adam asked, furrowing his eyebrows in concentration. "Only two hundred *thousand*?"

"Yes, give or take a few thousand," Yeva answered.

Keller grabbed Adam's shoulder and said, "I don't get it, what does that mean?"

Adam stared into empty space, thinking. "That turns everything on its head, but it explains a lot. The timeframe coincides with the sudden development of *Homo sapiens* on Earth."

"*Us*," Adam and Kellersaid simultaneously.

Adam started pacing. "So, Yeva, the Martian culture was having problems and sent explorers to *our* planet at around the same time modern humans appeared on Earth, crowding out the other subspecies? And the Martians waited for their explorers to return?"

"That seems to be correct," Yeva replied. "That is what the report from the NSA says. It looks like their explorers never returned home."

Adam grinned at Keller and said, "I think *we* just fulfilled that promise."

They both stood there with their mouths agape, trying to comprehend all of this new information.

"If that message is correct, then that explains a lot about our own history," Adam said.

There was silence from everybody.

"Yeva...," he continued. "Has the NSA deciphered what the creation was that caused the Martian's demise?"

"No. The university language expert said that the concept, as written, has no translation in either English or Russian. At least not yet. Whatever it was, they were very proud of it. Don't worry, we have hundreds of world experts trying to figure it out."

Adam sighed. "Okay. Thanks for the update, Yeva. That's a pretty heavy message. Um..., we're gonna keep working here for about another twenty minutes or so."

"*Okay, guys. Be safe out there,*" Yeva said before signing off.

The two explorers walked back to the anti-gravity cube room. They continued trying to photograph every granite panel they could see. The engravings went from the floor up to about ten feet and stopped. It would require a lot of photos to capture every detail.

When they finished taking pictures, Adam collected the memory cards from the cameras. He put them securely into his pressure suit pocket and zipped it shut.

Rather than leave right away, they began to play with the anti-gravity cube. For such an advanced piece of technology, it sure was fun. Just as Keller flicked it with his index finger, the ground began to shake just like it had done before. The floodlight tripod rocked back and forth, sending shadows bouncing on every wall.

Another Marsquake, Adam thought.

They felt a grinding vibration through the floor,

followed by a *clunk*. Dust fell from the ceiling and toppled down the walls. The floodlight stopped rocking. Everything sat still.

Adam and Keller looked at each other, frozen in fear.

The two astronauts ran toward the door. Their helmet-mounted flashlight beams bounced erratically, illuminating the ground, the ceiling, then back again. There was no light coming through the door opening anymore. The round slab of granite had rolled back over the entrance.

They were trapped.

CHAPTER 19

Big Turtle Housing Unit
Mars Landing Site

In the middle of the Big Turtle housing unit sat an inexplicable round wall. It was only about six feet in diameter, but there it was like a giant redwood tree growing up through the room. This round enclosure was the droppable caisson room. It was a hollow elevator shaft of sorts, sealed everywhere except the bottom. At the top were windows to allow ambient sunlight in. On one side was a hatch that would allow access to the empty enclosure after it lowered. The entire contraption resembled an upside down cup.

Any poor astronaut who wandered through that caisson door right now would instantly be exposed to the Martian atmosphere. They would fall out the bottom of the ship to their death.

Molly was listening to Yeva explain the NSA report over the microphone to Adam and Keller.

"*Okay, guys. Be safe out there,*" Yeva said.

She put down the printed report from the NSA.

"Adam and Keller are busy at the pyramid. I think we should lower the caisson and get some core samples," Yeva commanded.

"Of course. Let's play in the dirt," Molly replied.

With the flick of a few switches, the caisson started lowering toward the red soil very slowly; a low-frequency whirring sound filled the Big Turtle.

Molly and Yeva were surprised at how much the moving caisson momentarily shook the entire Big Turtle vehicle. However, it didn't shake very long. With a loud *clunk*, the caisson's bottom hit the ground and drove into it a few inches, powered by the entire weight of the Big Turtle on top of it. The whole building trembled momentarily.

Yeva typed a code into the wall computer near the caisson hatch. With the caisson floor now sealed off by Mars itself, this new outdoor room with a sandy red floor was slowly flooded with breathable air.

Yeva checked a few old-style "steam" gauges and declared, "Pressure looks good. The temperature is still a bit cold, though. Let us give it a minute."

The pressurization process was loud. *Everything* about the caisson was loud.

Yeva plastered her nose to the observation window looking down into the brightly lit cylindrical room. It was surreal to see the red dirt with shadows cast across it from the skylight window-frames above.

The temperature in the caisson finally rose to just above

freezing. Humid air was injected into the chamber to keep dust levels down. Yeva grabbed ahold of the big round door handle and spun it repeatedly. Once the mechanism let go, a wisp of air escaped through the opening into the caisson — a filtration system at the top made sure that fresh air kept coming into the caisson.

Yeva held her breath, stuck her head through the hatch, and looked down. Red dusty dirt. Yeva took in a deep breath hoping to get the first sense of what Mars smelled like. It smelled like rust with a touch of rotten egg. She grimaced. Each dramatic exhale of the cold air now sent a cloud of condensation from her lungs.

"Hey, Molly, this looks like plain red dirt to me," Yeva said jokingly.

She swung her legs through the hatch and began climbing down the ladder. Carefully at first, then quickly. When Yeva got to the bottom rung, she paused. She bit her lip in concentration and took the final step down to the dirt. It was much softer than she expected. It was like very dehydrated and powdery soil back on Earth. A huge grin overtook her face.

Yeva pulled a pair of nitrile gloves out of her pocket and was about to put them on, but paused. She bent down and scooped up a handful of the red soil. She stood up, holding it cupped in her hand. It was still so cold. No words could describe her childlike amazement. She was the first human to *touch* Mars, but nobody would notice. For reasons that not even she understood, Yeva brought her hand to her face and sniffed the red dirt. Something in it made her sinuses burn like a jolt of spicy Wasabi mustard. She cringed, but the burn didn't last long. After a few seconds, she turned her hand over and dumped the dusty stream of dirt to the ground. She wiped her hands together to get rid of any lingering dust.

Yeva began walking around the circular extent of the room, taking small steps at first. She looked down and saw the shoeprints she was leaving. Yeva stopped to contemplate an idea she was hatching. At that moment, she started hopping up and down on her right foot while removing her boot and sock from her left foot. She was now standing on her right leg and slowly dropped her foot on the soft red Martian soil. She laughed out loud.

Yeva dug her toes into the powdery dirt, then looked up to see Molly's head in the hatch looking down and laughing at her.

"You look like you're having way too much fun down there," Molly said with a concerned smile.

Yeva removed her other boot and sock and began to walk in circles around the room. The ground was painfully cold. Her walking was conjuring up a cloud of red dust now, but the condensation kept it low. Each breath sent out huge billowing clouds of condensation.

"Adam may have put the first shoeprint on Mars," Yeva yelled up to Molly, "but I am the first human to truly walk on this devil planet. I have touched it with my own feet!"

Yeva could only take the cold for so long, though. She put boots back on her nearly frostbitten feet and climbed back into the housing unit to warm up.

Yeva and Molly gathered several items of test equipment and took them through the hatch, one by one, and down the ladder. While Molly brought down more equipment, Yeva began setting up the machines.

First up were the portable spectrometer, seismic

sensors, and a whole host of compact soil study test kits. The tallest device looked like a standup vacuum cleaner, but it housed a core drilling machine that would take a meter-deep core sample of Martian soil and rock.

After Molly delivered the last test unit, Yeva asked her to help run the core drilling machine.

Molly nodded.

"Hold on," she said. "We need some work tunes."

She climbed up the ladder and disappeared through the hatch. Molly went over to the communications laptop and turned up the volume on the streaming music service so they could hear it in the caisson. She laughed, considering that a multi-million dollar interplanetary data link was being used to stream *Hotel California* to the speaker system on the ship.

Molly climbed down the ladder and the two of them began running their experiments and tests. In the room above them, Adam's garbled calls for help rang from the headset. For a brief moment, Yeva thought she heard something and paused, looking upward. A beeping sound from the core-drilling machine grabbed her attention. It finished extracting the first meter-long cylinder of rock. The machine cover popped open, revealing the entire extracted core.

"Oh my goodness," Yeva said with a huge grin.

The upper half of the core showed sand, rock, and powdery ice — just as expected. However, the lower half was full of fossilized sea-life deposits, somewhat similar to those found in ancient seafloors back on Earth. It had a mixture of familiar seashells and tube-like crinoids, but it also had a few dimpled shells that were just unusual enough to trigger their curiosity.

While they examined the treasured find, Molly thought she heard an unusual sound above the din of the music and looked upward. Unfortunately, Adam's pleas weren't loud enough to overcome the classic rock songs from the 1970's.

CHAPTER 20

Inside The Pyramid Structure

"Stop breathing!" Adam yelled at a panicking Keller.

"What do you mean, *stop breathing*!"

Adam closed his eyes to concentrate.

"I mean stop breathing *so fast*. Look, we have plenty of oxygen in our tanks, but there's no need to use it all up right now!"

Keller was clawing at the multi-ton door even though there was no way for him to move it. It hadn't closed all the way. There was still enough room to stick a few fingers through — perhaps enough to pry it open if they had a prybar.

"Too bad we don't have a *prybar*," Adam complained.

He looked around to see what they could use, but the only thing in the room aside from granite was the floodlight on a tripod and two digital cameras.

Adam turned on his headset and screamed, "Yeva! Molly! We need help! The door closed, and we're trapped!"

Only silence came back.

"I don't get it," he continued. "The door shouldn't completely block our signal."

"What are we going to do now?" Keller asked.

Adam turned toward Keller. "Nothing. We wait. That's all we can do."

Keller sat down on the floor and proceeded to breathe heavily again as his stress levels skyrocketed.

Adam ran over to Keller. "Look, you've gotta calm down," Adam begged. "If you keep breathing like that, you're going to run out of air."

Keller checked his gauge and looked back at Adam.

"I only have ten minutes left," Keller admitted, with panic in his eyes.

Adam looked at his own gauge and saw he had nearly twenty minutes left. Keller was using up his air too quickly. Without thinking, Adam blurted out, "Keller, did you bring your pills?"

"With me? Are you mental? What am I going to do? Rip off my helmet and slam down some meds with a handful of my own pee?"

Adam paced back and forth. "Look, I don't know. Okay, you gotta slow down that breathing. Don't worry. They will come for us."

Adam plopped down on the ground next to Keller.

"Think of your happiest memory."

"What? Are you serious?" Keller asked incredulously.

"Look, I'm trying to calm us down. Tell me your favorite memory," Adam demanded.

Keller stared at him. "No."

Silence followed as Adam stood back up and wandered around the room looking for something that could help them out of this trouble.

Keller sat there shaking. He turned to look at Adam and said pathetically, "Okay, I'll try it *your* way."

Adam walked back toward him.

"It's about the world's tallest tree," Keller continued. "Look, I'm telling you — this is pointless."

"Just do it," Adam scolded. "Okay? Now tell me about the world's tallest tree."

Keller grinned slightly. "Yeah, all right. Some of my high-school friends and I were competing in this big contest to have the world's fastest bicycle. Every bike had a fancy aerodynamic shroud around it. This was back in the 1990's — *1994* I think. Yeah, our whole team went out to the big race in California. Well, we crashed our bike on the first practice run, so we had like three days to kill before the flight home."

Adam sensed that Keller was slowing down his breathing.

"So we decide to go see the world's tallest tree. It's up around a town called Eureka, you know, in northern California. Anyway, we drive way up this mountain. Like 45 minutes. We get to the entrance gate at the park where the tree is. It's got a combination lock on it."

Adam laughed. "And you didn't have the combination, right?"

"That's right," Keller confirmed. "Turns out you have to pay for access before you drive all the way up that mountain and they were closed by the time we got there. So we're parked there in the middle of nowhere wondering what to do. Then we see a car coming up to the locked gate from the *other* side — they were just at the world's tallest tree!"

Keller laughed.

"It's like a three mile drive from that gate down a gravel road to the tree. So the car stops and it's a family visiting from Korea. The Dad can't get the lock undone, so, like he can't leave the park! He sees us young punks there and asks us for help. So he gives *us* the combination, and we open the gate for him. When they leave, we re-open the gate and drive down that gravel road. We saw that tree. Yes we did."

Keller could remember the scene clearly. He was back there. It was 1994. He was listening to the new Pink Floyd album on his Walkman. It was the highlight of his teenage years.

"Okay, Captain Alston, what is *your* favorite memory?"

Adam contemplated and smiled as his mind flooded with memories of happier times.

"I guess I have *two*, really. The first is listening to music with my kids in the living room on a warm Texas summer day. So, one day, my daughter is standing on my toes, and we're dancing around the living room to the 'Rainbow Connection' song. You know, that Muppets song? The one that goes '*Someday we'll find it, the rainbow connection*'?"

Adam could almost hear Kermit's voice singing to the banjo as he and his daughter danced in the dusty sunbeams flooding through the big arched windows in the living room.

Keller laughed out loud. "Yes, I remember that song."

Adam looked wistfully at the ground. "I guess that's more of a scene really. Not much story there, huh? Now, I also have a memory of being a kid watching MacGyver with my family and —"

"Oh crap, oh no!" Keller cried, looking over at Adam.

"Well, I know it's not a *tallest tree* story, but give me some credit," Adam replied sheepishly.

"No, no. It's not that," Keller said. He had a look of realization and surprise on his face. "We've got the golf cart. Yeva and Molly have no way to get here. They could walk, but they'd never make it in time."

Adam knew that already and was hoping Keller wouldn't realize it until after he calmed down. Now, Adam was panicking because Keller was panicking.

The rescuers that they were counting on wouldn't make it here in time. They *couldn't* make it here in time. Their doom was becoming certain. Adam's brain went into overdrive. He started making fists to crack his knuckles; it helped his brain work during stressful times.

"Think, think, think," he said out loud.

He looked at Keller and asked, "How much oxygen do you have now?"

Keller looked down at his gauge.

"About seven minutes."

Adam stopped pacing. "Okay, look, we're desperate. We've got one chance here. We do have *something* that might move that door, but one of us will have to hold our breath."

"What in the world are you talking about?" Keller blurted out.

"These oxygen bottles we have on our backs," Adam explained. "If we knock the nozzle off, the oxygen will shoot out fast and act like a rocket of sorts, pushing on the door. At least for a few seconds."

"Then we both die from suffocation. *Nice plan,*" Keller complained sarcastically.

Adam shook his head.

"No, we'll only use one tank. We have an auxiliary Y-hose so we can share the remaining tank with each other."

"Okay, use my tank," Keller said. "It's almost empty."

Adam looked at him with distressed eyes.

"No, Keller. We have to use the one with the *most* oxygen. It'll pack the biggest punch."

"That means...," Keller said, afraid to finish his own thought.

Adam ran back to the anti-gravity cube room and grabbed the floodlight. He brought it back to the door and placed it on the ground. He reached down and pulled out the hammer that was in a pocket on his pressure suit.

Adam looked at Keller and asked, "Are you ready? We'll have to run like crazy when this door falls down."

"Or die if it doesn't," Keller said.

Adam reached back to disconnect his oxygen tank, but hesitated. Instead, he talked into his headset microphone, "Yeva? Molly? Can you hear me? Hey look, we're trapped in the pyramid. The door rolled back over the opening. We're going to try to knock the door over with one of our oxygen tanks, but it probably won't work. If you get this message, please bring us oxygen. I'm not sure how, but please try."

Adam looked at Keller and said, "Let me explain what I'm going to do. I'll remove my oxygen tank, and *you* hold it up against the door — up near the top. Wedge it against the door jamb if you have to. Do not let go of the tank! When I knock the nozzle off, that rocket power should push on the top of the door. That may be enough force to make it tumble outward. Got it?"

Keller nodded in nervous agreement.

Adam looked for courage. He squeezed his eyes shut and thought of dancing in the sunbeams with his daughter again. He smiled at the memory as he gulped in some air and held his breath. With the hammer in his right hand, he reached back with his left hand and disconnected the tank from his backpack.

The tank fell off onto the ground. Adam grabbed it and jammed it against the top of the door. Keller held it in place with both gloves. Adam got a good grip on the hammer. He swung at the nozzle and hit it with authority. It bent sideways, but didn't break.

Adam reached back and swung again. He missed and smashed Keller's thumb. Keller let out a guttural scream, but he didn't let go of the tank. Now panicked, Adam swung back hard and the hammer flew out of his grip, spinning off into the darkness.

Adam's eyes bulged in terror, his heart racing. He took another breath of the remaining oxygen in his suit and quickly looked around the nearby floor. No sign of a hammer.

Adam fell to the floor to run his hands through the dirt to find it. He stood up and ran off into the darkness, but still couldn't find it among the dusty ground covering. He looked up and noticed Keller was frozen with fear.

Adam ran back toward the door and grabbed one of the digital cameras and smashed it against the bent tank valve. Camera bits went everywhere, but the tank nozzle remained intact. Adam dropped to his knees knowing that he only had another minute of consciousness left. A silence came over him even though his heart was still pounding. Hypoxia was setting in.

Adam felt something tap him on the shoulder. He looked up. Keller was holding the bottle up with one hand

and pointing his other toward the darkened room with the anti-gravity cube.

"Get the cube!" Keller yelled over the headset.

Adam jumped to his feet and ran into the darkness, his path illuminated by his head-mounted flashlight. He grabbed the cube and ran back toward the door. The cube was a mixture of strangeness. It seemed unusually dense for its size, almost made out of something as heavy as gold. Adam lifted the cube with both hands and smashed it down on the bent tank nozzle.

A roar came out of the tank as it jack-hammered into the big granite door. Keller could barely hold the tank as it jittered wildly around the top of the door jamb, but finally the big stone door slowly leaned away from the pyramid. The oxygen bottle rocketed for only a few more seconds, but at the last moment, the door toppled away from them with a ground-rattling thud, revealing bright sunshine and the golf cart in the distance.

Adam fell down with suffocation. He was on all fours with no strength to stand. His hand reached into one of his suit utility pockets and pulled out an auxiliary Y-shaped air hose. He feebly held it up to Keller for him to share his remaining air.

"*No*," Keller said over the headset.

Adam looked at Keller in horror.

"What? Hook me up!" Adam demanded. " I'm dying!"

Keller looked at his oxygen gauge.

"I know. But I've only got four minutes left. If I share this," he gulped. "Neither of us will make it back to the ship alive."

Adam's eyes filled with bloodshot rage.

Keller's face betrayed the guilt he felt for his decision. He chose to abandon the man who had led him and two others safety to Mars — the first manned mission.

"I'm sorry, Adam. Look, I'm really sorry. I'll... I'll tell everybody that you died a hero," Keller said. "We'll bury you here on Mars, okay?"

Adam gasped for air like a helpless fish out of its tank. Keller turned away. "I know you saved my life back there, Adam, but I gotta go right now."

Adam's vision began to blur, the colors of Mars fading to black and white. All he could see out of his visor was the floodlight tripod.

Keller stumbled toward the golf cart, pausing a few feet away to catch his breath. He slumped over with hands on knees; resting for just a second, trying to calm down his racing heart, no doubt caused by the explosion of guilt he felt for his friend.

Adam reached out a trembling hand and grabbed the floodlight tripod. He pushed through all his pain and light-headedness to stand up, climbing the tripod like a crutch. He stumbled up behind Keller and with his last remaining strength, swung the tripod like a baseball bat right into Keller's helmet, shattering open the glass on his visor.

Keller fell to the ground and did not move — his last breath was now part of the billowing Mars breeze. A crackle of ice formed over his eyes, stuck wide open and opaque Adam rolled Keller's body onto his side and unlatched the coveted oxygen tank.

"I'm sorry, Keller. I've got a family that depends on me. *You don't.*"

CHAPTER 21

A lone astronaut jogged across the surface of Mars beneath the grayish maroon sky. Each step kicked up a red cloud. Her footsteps led directly from the Big Turtle. She was clearly following the tire tracks left by the multiple golf cart trips. "Don't slow down now!" she said to herself with labored breaths. "Molly, this is where all those years of jogging pays off! Keep going!"

She dragged behind her the only extra oxygen tank they had that was full — otherwise Yeva would have been with her. Molly held a crowbar in her left hand. She had heard the crackly final message left by Adam and was racing to the pyramid to see if she could save them.

Molly paused and bent over to catch her breath. A reflection in her visor made her look up. She saw a fountain of red dust in the distance. It was getting taller. And closer.

After a few moments, she saw the golf cart racing toward her. Molly squinted and saw there was only one person sitting in it. She waved at it to stop, but it continued full speed toward her.

As the golf cart came closer, Molly saw it swerving erratically, trying to follow the old tire tracks. It looked like a drunk driver was handling it. The driver wasn't slowing down, either.

Molly jumped out of the way to keep from getting hit. A shower of red sand and grit fell on her as the golf cart passed by and kept going.

"Hey, Yeva, this is Molly. I'm halfway there and the golf cart just drove past me toward Big Turtle. Somebody is driving toward you fast."

"Then you should come back, too," Yeva replied.

"But there was only one person in the cart. Should I continue on to the pyramid just in case?"

Yeva didn't reply. Her silence acknowledged what they were both thinking.

"If there was only one person driving," Yeva said, about to state the obvious. "I assume the other one is dead. You should come back now."

Molly felt like she'd been punched in the gut and started to hyperventilate. "Please, dear God, let it be Keller in the golf cart," she whispered in her helmet.

The golf cart continued racing through the Martian dust and grit. Adam could no longer see in color; only brief images in black and white as he dazed in and out of consciousness. He saw the Big Turtle and knew that he had to get near the door. He misjudged the distance and crashed it into the side of the ramp, sending a jolt through the entire Big Turtle. He was thrown out of the vehicle and landed near one of the Big Turtle's support legs.

Adam crawled up the ramp and into the airlock. He

forcefully grabbed each of his legs and pulled them into the little room. He yanked the outside door shut. Adam could hear the air flooding in as Yeva spun the valves to help pressurize it quickly. He ripped off his helmet and gasped the deepest breath of his life. The tunnel vision subsided, but he still couldn't see colors. The door to the ship interior flew open.

"Where is Keller!" Yeva screamed. "Why isn't he with you? What happened?"

Adam reached up toward her with his hand, but it fell down again. He was gasping heavily now and eked out a pathetic, "Keller... he... we..."

He gulped another huge breath of air.

"We got trapped, and..."

Adam was hyperventilating. His vision went blurry.

"He didn't. He, uh. Keller... he..."

Adam passed out. His head slumped to the floor.

CHAPTER 22

Adam's eyes popped open. It was dark. No sunshine came through the windows.

It must be the middle of the night, he thought. *How much time had passed?*

He felt around in the darkness. He must be lying in the medical bed. Sensor cables dangled from his temples.

Adam swung his legs carefully out of bed, letting his feet gently touch the cold floor. He stood up, trying to clear his foggy brain.

Was it a dream, he asked himself. Adam looked over at the bed stations. Yeva and Molly were there, but Keller's bed was empty.

"Oh no," he whispered.

His lungs still hurt. He shuffled over to the communication station, careful not to pull the wires from his sensors. There was a light blinking near the microphone. That meant they had a message from Mission Control. He looked back to make sure everybody was asleep. Adam put on the headphones and pushed the play button.

"Okay crew, this is Chris Tankovitch. We heard about the terrible news. I am sorry you have to deal with this. Keller's assistant Lydia has been notified, but we haven't made any public announcements. We just had an emergency meeting and you'll have to bury him there. Without refrigeration it wouldn't be safe to keep him in either the housing unit or the return capsule. And you just can't strap him to the outside of the ship."

Adam considered the grim task ahead and cringed.

The message from Chris continued, "You'll have to play it by ear, but do the best you can. So far, we think you should continue the mission until completion, but that's up to you. Oh, and Molly, we received the uploaded photos from Adam and Keller's investigation of that floating cube thing. Unfortunately, the video upload from Adam's helmet is taking a really long time. Just let it run overnight. We'll review it when it's finished."

Adam suddenly froze with fear. His pulse skyrocketed. The health monitoring computer he was hooked up to started beeping.

"Crap!" he said.

Adam tried to think happy thoughts. Quickly. Sun beams! Sun beams! His pulse calmed down, and the beeping stopped. Yeva and Molly didn't wake up.

He searched the desktop and found the battered helmet

that he'd worn on the mission. The upload cable was plugged into the video camera port. The light was blinking which meant the upload was still in progress. Adam reached over and yanked out the cable. In the brief moments of lucidity during the wild drive back, he had hoped to discuss the event with his crew and Mission Control before they watched the helmet video. That was unlikely to happen now. Adam had no idea how much video Mission Control had already received.

Suddenly, bright light from the sunrise tore through the window edges and lit up the room with a dull gray glow. It was morning on Mars. The automatic blinds slowly rolled up.

Adam tiptoed back to the medical bed and laid back down to think over the recent events. Ten minutes later, the morning wakeup call came from their ship computer. It was a mechanical voice saying, "Rise and shine!" The voice was way too happy for the mood on Mars. Molly and Yeva slowly stirred from their sleep and woke up. Adam stood up and put together breakfast for everybody.

Yeva was the first to show; Molly was in the bathroom. Yeva looked around to make sure Molly couldn't hear her.

"Molly isn't doing so well," she whispered to Adam. "She's very upset. Frankly, we've both been too upset to even watch the video. Be careful what you say to her, okay?"

Adam nodded without making eye contact.

They sat down to their bland tubes of raisin bran and coffee. However, nobody had much of an appetite.

"Adam, please tell us what happened out there," Yeva said, breaking the silence.

Adam took a drink of coffee and stared at the table.

"A Marsquake caused the door to close on us. We were

stuck inside. In order to get out, we used one of our oxygen tanks as an air hammer to knock the door down."

Adam looked up at their intense faces.

He added, "We were down to one tank without enough air for both of us. And then I, *we*, had to make a terrible decision."

Molly started to cry loudly.

"He gave up his life for you?" she asked through the sobbing.

"Yes. He saved my life," Adam said plainly.

She was leaning on the table with her hands covering her face, still crying loudly.

That was all Adam was willing to say. The head-mounted video camera didn't record sound. Instead, their microphone dialogue was transmitted to the receivers on the Big Turtle and relayed to Houston; later spliced with the video by NASA personnel. Unfortunately, they didn't receive any usable audio from the time they were trapped. Without hearing the actual words exchanged between them in the pyramid, Adam realized that his description of the events would eventually be questioned. He hoped that someday his own explanation would add context to the unfortunate video. He wondered how much Chris had watched of the video, if any.

Molly was trying to slow down her tears. Her nose was pouring snot.

"Look, I understand this is an awful thing," Adam said, trying to calm her. "He died a hero. I'll go back to the pyramid today and get him, okay? We'll give him a proper burial with full honors."

"You broke the golf cart during your trip back," Yeva

explained. "You will have to go there on foot."

Adam sighed and nodded — bad news after bad news.

He got up and hugged Molly. "I'm so sorry this happened."

Adam walked over to the medical bed, sat down, and turned away from the two women. He was incapable of processing anything else right now. All he could think about was having a video-conference with his family, but that would have to wait a few more hours.

Late morning finally arrived and Adam suited up for his long workday. He had three tasks when he got outside. First, see if the golf cart was easily repairable. It wasn't. Second, dig a grave. Below the dusty surface, the ground was compacted and very hard to dig. The digging process took him so long that he had to replace his oxygen tank.

Now, for his final task. Walk to the pyramid and retrieve not only Keller, but the anti-gravity cube that he'd left. It would most likely be his last trip to the pyramid. Getting home was all he cared about now.

Adam followed the golf cart tracks as well as Molly's bootprints from the day before. It was going to be the longest walk of his life. Not in time or distance, but in the cost to his spirit. He had faced a life or death decision, and he chose life — a decision may have cost him his soul.

Before Adam got too far, his headset buzzed, "Wait up! I am coming with you."

The airlock opened and Yeva emerged. Each of them wore fresh oxygen tanks for this long walk. It took nearly twenty minutes to reach the fossil site. Neither one said a word. They walked past the fossil boulders and toward the pyramid. Adam noticed the wheel tracks left by the Curiosity and saw what direction it had taken the day before. He slowed down as he approached the pyramid.

Yeva stopped when she saw Keller's body in the distance. It was facing down in the red dust.

"You stay here," Adam said. "I'll go take care of him."

He walked over and laid out the body bag. NASA included them on all of their missions, but had never had to use one until now. He rolled Keller's body into it and zipped it up most of the way. Adam stopped briefly to look at the helmet. He saw a gruesome face through the missing visor glass. Keller's expression was frozen solid, literally and emotionally — his eyes frosted over in shock. Adam looked away as he zipped the body bag completely closed.

Yeva looked curiously at the floodlight tripod. It was broken open and laying just a few feet away.

Adam stood up. "Let's go get the anti-gravity cube. I'll show you what it does when we get back to the Big Turtle."

They walked past the toppled door and into the pyramid. The room was heavily illuminated by sunlight. Adam found the anti-gravity cube floating over near a wall. He picked it up and was still amazed at how dense it felt. With nowhere on his suit to store it, he walked back outside and placed it in the body bag with Keller. Adam tied a bungee cord to the bag and tied the other end to his pressure suit. With the low gravity on Mars, it wouldn't be very difficult to pull it back to the Big Turtle.

"Let's head home," Adam said.

He didn't complain about having to drag the load all the way back to the Big Turtle. Once again, nobody spoke. As they approached the base, they noticed that Molly had decided to join them. She was next to the gravesite, kneeling down to look into the freshly dug hole.

Adam knew that Molly had grown close to Keller during the training in California; they were unofficially a couple that neither he nor Yeva told NASA about. Keller's death was hard on her.

In between these somber thoughts, Adam remembered that he and Yeva had taken all of the full oxygen tanks with them. Molly didn't have one.

CHAPTER 23

Molly had had a simple reaction to the news about Keller. It hit her like a freight train. Part of her very being perished that morning in slow motion; her soul followed soon after. It was a mortal wound. After Adam and Yeva left to retrieve Keller's body, Molly put on her pressure suit, neglecting to notice or care that it had no oxygen tank. She exited through the airlock and walked over to the gravesite that Adam had created. She knelt down in front of the empty hole. Molly thought about Keller as she slowly consumed all of the remaining oxygen in her suit. She grew light headed. She didn't fall over. She just sat in that position. By the time Adam and Yeva found her, she was frozen solid in a position of eternal mourning.

Yeva started sobbing uncontrollably. Her helmet was fogging up. She ran over to Molly's lifeless body, wanting to help, but realized there was nothing she could do.

Adam let go of the body bag and ran over to Yeva.

"I should've stayed with her," Yeva cried.

"Look Yeva, we're all under tremendous stress. You

couldn't have known she would do something like this."

She swung around in impatient anger.

"But I should've known!" Yeva yelled.

"What do you mean?" Adam asked, confused.

Yeva closed her eyes. "Do you remember back during the training in California? You thought Keller and Molly were getting a little too close and it might jeopardize the mission?"

"Yes, we both remember that," Adam admitted.

"Well, you were right on all counts. You should've said something to them! During the initial launch up to the Space Station, do you remember her vomiting in her helmet?"

"Yeah, she got motion sickness. I did too. It's common."

Yeva gained her composure back and stared blankly at Adam. She delicately shook her head side to side.

"No. Molly told me it was *morning sickness*. It was the first time she'd ever had it."

Adam collapsed, his mouth agape. He leaned on the shovel that was sticking out of the dirt.

Yeva looked down at him.

"I take it you didn't know?" Yeva asked.

"No, of course not," Adam replied, shaking his head. "I just assumed she was gaining weight."

"Oh my God, are you serious?" Yeva asked with a look of disbelief and horror.

"Look, the *alternative* was unthinkable, right?"

"Unfortunately, the alternative was *true*. She didn't even know for sure until after we'd left the Space Station. There was no turning back."

With a lump in his throat, Adam asked, "Who knew?"

"She told Chris Tankovitch. About a week after we

launched, he raised some questions about her medical readings. Chris decided against releasing the information to the public. Not until our return."

Adam looked up at Yeva, his eyes wide open.

"Did Keller know?"

"Yes, she told him right before you guys left for the pyramid."

Silence.

Adam was reprocessing all that had happened. After a minute, he broke the quiet with an offer for Yeva.

"That's really..., that's some pretty awful news. I need some time to think. Look, you go inside, and I'll dig another grave. Right next to Keller."

Yeva shook her head. "You know what, I would rather stay here with you for a while."

Adam took the shovel and started the arduous task of digging another hole in the hard sand and loose bedrock. He couldn't help but thinking that he was actually digging graves for three people. Adam considered joining them.

Each shovel of dirt weighed more and more. It took longer than he wanted, but he didn't care. He put Molly gently down in the new grave and slowly covered her in Martian sand and gravel. He carefully put Keller in his grave and started shoveling dirt on top of him. Halfway through, he halted, remembering that the anti-gravity cube was still in the body bag.

Oh no, he thought.

Adam unzipped the body bag and removed the anti-gravity cube. He zipped the bag back up and finished the burial. The dry red dust swirled around as he shoveled one last scoop of dirt on top of the bodies.

Adam found the American and Russian flags they had planted early on and built a makeshift cross out of them, connecting them with some thin nylon rope from the golf cart toolkit. He stuck the cross in the ground between the graves. Adam said a quick prayer and asked for forgiveness.

Yeva didn't say a word. She turned and walked up the dented ramp. She paused, tilting her head to figure out what was wrong with the airlock. She could see straight through it.

"Hey, Adam?"

He paused to lean on the shovel and look at her.

"Yes, Yeva?"

"Both ends of the airlock are wide open. I don't think Molly bothered to close them when she came outside."

Adam swung his head around quickly.

"Oh no, the air must all be gone by now!" Adam yelled.

Yeva ran through the airlock, quickly followed by Adam. He grabbed both doors and slammed them shut. The inside of Big Turtle was at a near vacuum. The temperature had dropped to nearly -100 degrees Fahrenheit.

Adam, returning to panic mode, stated the obvious, "We can't take our helmets off, and neither of us has much air!"

"Calm down, Adam. First thing's first. We already sealed the door. Now, go over to the life support panel and crank up the oxygen generation system — if it still works."

Adam sprinted over to the panel, but slipped and fell, smashing his helmet on the dinner table. The water supplies had exploded and frozen over, leaving an ice sheet on the floor. Adam heard a hissing sound coming from a growing crack in his facemask.

"Oh, please, please no!" he yelled as he stood back up and speed-walked over to the life support panel.

Adam grabbed the oxygen system knob and cranked it up to its maximum. That would hopefully make the room breathable in a few minutes. Adam tried to focus his eyes on the crack in his visor, only three inches from his face. His gloved hand came up against the crack to help slow the leak.

That was enough to avoid disaster. The ship was finally pressurizing with a mix of nitrogen and oxygen.

Adam looked down the hallway connecting them to Little Turtle and noticed the door was shut. "It looks like we had a bit of good luck for a change. Look over there, the door to the Little Turtle is shut. Our return supplies are probably still undamaged by the extreme temperatures. Maybe Molly was telling us to go home."

When the Big Turtle was done pressurizing, Adam wandered toward the return ship and investigated. He opened the door and walked in, closing the door behind him to keep in some of the heat. The water was still liquid. He breathed a sigh of relief. He cranked up the heaters on the entire complex to prevent any more disasters.

Yeva took an inventory of their food supplies. The food was fine, but half of their water bags had exploded from the cold.

Yeva stood up after reviewing the water situation and said, "Looks like our departure deadline has been moved up quite a bit."

After a few minutes, they took off their helmets.

"It's still pretty cold,"Yeva admitted, "but we are so lucky that our oxygen generators weren't damaged. Good God that was close. I hate to think what else is broken that we don't know about yet."

She noticed that the communication-station light was

blinking again. There was a message waiting for them. Yeva pushed the Play button.

"Guys, this is Chris Tankovitch again. Hello? Look, we need you to talk to us. I realize things are crazy up there with Keller gone, but we've got a real public relations nightmare happening down here. One of our heroes is dead, and the rest of you guys are AWOL. You need to contact us. Molly, check your medical sensors. Something is wrong with them. Try to reset them. Adam, I need you to contact us in private, okay? We have some quick questions to ask you."

Adam could imagine what their questions would be about. Talking to Mission Control was the last thing he wanted to do right now.

The Sun set and gray redness draped across the landscape. The salmon-colored sky had evolved into the violet and dark tones of the evening. The two astronauts decided they would sleep through the quickly oncoming night and send Mission Control the terrible news about Molly in the morning. Adam would get one more night of sleep while still a hero to his family.

There would be plenty of time to become a villain.

They started the streaming music service and decided on something quiet and peaceful. After the ten minute wait for the data to start streaming from Earth, calming Mozart melodies began pouring from the speakers.

Adam climbed into bed and heard a crinkle sound beneath his pillow. He reached under it and found a piece of paper with a note signed by Molly. It said, "I watched your helmet video."

CHAPTER 24

International Space Station
Orbiting Earth

Life on board the International Space Station slowed down once the Mars astronauts were gone. The media stopped paying attention to them as soon as the astronauts and their Little Turtle launched toward the Red Planet.

Frankly, there wasn't much left for the Mars support crew to do on the Space Station. In between playing poker with magnetic cards on a metal table, they tended to the occasional maintenance issues on the Storage Wart. It still hung from the ISS like some terrible growth. Every morning they had to make sure the large communication antennas were functioning properly. Without those, the crew on Mars would have a hard time communicating with Mission Control.

News of Keller's death made it to the ISS. A somber mood settled over the crew. Mission Control told them to continue doing their daily system checkups. In just one more week, a fresh crew of astronauts would arrive to relieve the current batch.

The two Storage Wart maintenance positions were manned by Larry and James, two astronauts from Boston and Mississippi, respectively. The Russian crewmembers on the Space Station had an ongoing contest regarding which American was harder to understand. Mississippi usually won.

The Storage Wart garnered very little attention from Mission Control. The daily routine consisted of going over endless checklists and turning off most of the power-hungry computers, except for the communications relay to Mars.

Just after midnight, an alarm was triggered. James opened his groggy eyes and hustled over to the status display readout. In red letters, it stated: RELAY #23 — OUTER STORAGE BOX-OVERVOLTAGE. The alarm was a series of loud beeps that were meant to be annoying. It worked. It woke Larry up too.

"What's going on?" Larry asked.

"You know that special auxiliary compartment on the outside of the Storage Wart? It looks like a relay in there may have shorted out. Unfortunately, we don't have a camera view in that box. We might have to get suited up."

They stared at each other wondering who would do the spacewalk; like two brothers staring at each other to determine who had to clean up the dog poop in the yard.

Larry had more experience with spacewalks, so he suited up and floated into the utility module where the airlock was. James heard a loud *clunk* which meant Larry had sealed himself into the airlock compartment.

"Okay, I'm in the airlock, it's evacuated," Larry said. "I'll be at the special auxiliary compartment in a minute." He opened the door and wandered outside the womblike protection of the Space Station.

James moved over to the porthole to get a better look at his crewmate outside. Larry clambered his way from the airlock exit over to the Storage Wart. James saw Larry's silhouette on the outside of the Space Station. He looked like a bug crawling on a milk jug. As the Sun peeked over the horizon of the Earth, Larry lit up as bright as a flare. This sunrise surprise happens every 90 minutes on the ISS.

Larry floated out to the far end of the Storage Wart where the large rectangular box was located — the box specially requested by the president himself. Larry was now out of view of James.

The special compartment was still closed, but a little bit of smoke wafted out. Larry was curious because nobody knew what type of equipment was installed in the compartment. He attached his safety tether to a metal anchor loop and twisted the big toggle-turn fasteners that kept the doors closed on the compartment.

The doors hinged open. They flexed back and forth as thin metal doors do. Larry's heart pounded as the blinding sunlight illuminated eight thermonuclear B61 bombs that had been converted to guided missiles. They were mounted on some type of spring-loaded ejection racks.

Larry remembered seeing this type of bomb for the first time when he worked in the Air Force as a crew member on bomber aircraft. These particular bombs, however, were modified from what he remembered: each one had a rocket motor attached to it along with a guidance system. The smoke came from a small white control box. It had cables running to *all eight* of the bomb ejectors. They were sparking.

Unbeknownst to the Space Station crew, the president and the Defense Department thought this orbiting missile launch platform might come in handy someday if an aggressor tried to put America in a military bind. It would reduce the time necessary to strike first, depending on where the International Space Station was at the time.

"Hey, do you see the problem?" James asked over the headset. "Is it a blown fuse?"

"Oh, I see the problem, all right," Larry answered in a shrill tone.

"What do you mean? What is it?"

"I think somebody in the Pentagon thought the Storage Wart would make a good permanent space-borne launch platform for nukes. There's enough destructive firepower here to start a new Hell."

James was confused. "What in the world are you talking about?"

"What I'm saying is... this auxiliary compartment on the Storage Wart is filled with rocket powered *bombs*. B61's I think. The *big-boom mushroom-cloud* kind. It looks like the ejector controller is sparking. Some kind of short circuit for sure. The wires all look chaffed; the protective insulation is scraped off. The bumpy ride up here must've ruined these control wires. Man, they built these modules too quickly."

"Sparking? Bombs? I think we should contact Mission Control."

"I don't think there's a checklist for this problem," Larry said, now even more tense.

His heart raced; his pulse pounded in his neck . He saw the smoke coming from the corner of the white ejector control box. Larry carefully grabbed onto one of the bomb fins for leverage. He reached up into the tight compartment trying to feel with his thick-gloved fingers. He managed to move a large spring loaded retainer clip from the cover of the white box, hoping to disconnect the power cable.

Suddenly, the control box exploded in a shower of sparks. All of the bomb ejectors fired off, sending a sharp mechanical jolt through the entire Space Station. Eight B61 thermonuclear bombs flew out of the compartment like a flock of doves thrown from a cage. The arming panels on each bomb lit up and came to life. The violent ejection ripped the glove from Larry's suit. The decompression happened so fast he didn't have time to scream out in pain. His radio crackled for a few seconds.

"Larry! Larry! What happened?" James cried out.

There was no response.

James planted his face to the observation window, trying to see what was happening. In the distance, Larry floated motionless at the end of the tether. Just past the body was a cluster of bombs sinking down toward Earth, silently and slowly. James screamed for the other astronauts to come help. When they finally arrived, they couldn't get James to calm down enough to tell them what happened.

The bombs floated down for a while until their rocket engines ignited. They took off in large curved trajectories toward targets in Russia, the default targets chosen long ago by some Pentagon committee that thought they'd never actually be used.

The other Space Station crew members floated to the nearest porthole windows to see what was happening. James stared helplessly out the window mouthing the words, "No, no, no!"

Large flashes appeared on the ground in Russia, each one growing its own mushroom cloud. James managed to engage the voice communication channel with Mission Control, yelling, "Tell the Russians not to retaliate! It was an accident!" Unfortunately, his voice was so loud that it squelched out any useful communication.

Suddenly, James went silent. He saw a swarm of retaliatory missiles launch from rural locations in Siberia, heading over the North Pole towards America. Each astronaut on the Space Station still had his face planted in one of the available portholes, with a view down to Earth. Minutes passed. More mushroom-cloud plumes appeared all over the blue and white planet below.

A buzzing alarm turned on.

Everybody's ears popped like a high-altitude airplane ride. The Space Station was losing air pressure.

The jolt from the bomb ejectors firing off had caused a leak between the Storage Wart and the rest of the station. The Wart was now killing its host. The International Space Station was losing pressure quickly, and electrical problems were plaguing their rescue attempts. The crew couldn't seal off the other compartments fast enough.

The captain, realizing that the station was doomed, got on the intercom and gave the signal three times, "Abandon ship. Abandon ship. Abandon ship."

The astronauts put on their pressure suits as fast as

they could. They made their way to the emergency escape vehicles and belted in. The doors closed and they started the release sequence.

The escape vehicles separated with a *clunk*. They floated quietly down toward Earth where visible mushroom clouds pockmarked the surface like big, deadly flowers. The crew looked out the big window in the roof of the vehicle toward the Space Station. The Storage Wart was shaking back and forth. It started to rotate. Finally, it ripped away from its mount completely. The International Space Station seemed to be flinging off an irritating pest.

CHAPTER 25

Big Turtle Housing Unit
Mars Landing Site

The streaming music stopped playing over the speakers on Big Turtle. That was the first sign that something was wrong. Alarms blared, one by one, ending in a crescendo of ear-splitting chaos.

Adam ran around clearing individual alarms, but the worry on his face grew more pronounced with each one. The ship was losing contact with Mission Control back home. The computer screen that normally listed the names of files being sent and received displayed a complaint, instead: "Lost server connection." On Earth, that error would just be annoying. On Mars, that error was unsettling.

Adam engaged the emergency backup communications channel — he heard nothing but pure silence. His stomach sank. The video screens filled with error messages. The laptops disconnected from the servers in Houston. No information was coming in.

The alarms woke Yeva up and she stumbled in.

"We're completely cut off," Adam fretted.

"What is going on?" she asked, rubbing her eyes.

"I don't know. We've lost all communication with Mission Control. We've got power, just no signal. No video. No audio. No data. *Nothing*."

The two explorers were completely isolated on a desolate planet, and they didn't know why.

"Have you tried the deep-space emergency frequencies?"

Adam nodded. "Yes, I've tried everything. Nothing's come back. We're just... cut off from Earth."

"What else could it be?" Yeva inquired.

Adam jogged over to the window and craned his neck upward, trying to see the long-range antenna sticking up out of the top of the Little Turtle. It was the main communication antenna between the two planets. If it had fallen over, that was something he could potentially fix. His heart sank.

It looks perfectly fine, he thought.

Adam ran back over to the communications station to check the data connection between Little Turtle's antenna and the orbiting communications-relay satellite.

It looks perfectly fine, too.

"Everything on our end is working," Adam said, frowning with concern. "The trouble must be on their side. Maybe the Space Station lost power? I guess we'll just have to wait until they get it fixed."

Adam sat down in the chair and eased back, letting his arms hang dejectedly. "I don't like this at all. Mission Control better get things fixed, or we're in big trouble."

He picked up the microphone and pushed the transmit button. "NASA, this is Big Turtle. We are transmitting into the blind here. We are not receiving any signals from you."

Adam glanced at Yeva for a moment and added, "However, we will continue with our mission duties. Just send us a message as soon as you can. We have all channels open, even the deep-space emergency frequencies."

Adam turned off the microphone and turned to Yeva. "They'll get that in five minutes and, hopefully, we'll get a reply back in ten."

His message was converted into electro-magnetic waves and transmitted from the tall long-range antenna protruding from the roof of the Little Turtle. Those signals beamed to the communications relay satellite orbiting Mars. It amplified the signals and retransmitted them toward Earth. Those signals travelled through space at the speed of light. They reached the abandoned and unpowered International Space Station five minutes later.

Inside the Big Turtle, anxiety levels were climbing. The pure silence fueled the tension.

"This mission is *cursed*," Yeva complained.

"I hope..." he trailed off. "I'm *sure* this is just a technical glitch. Look, the loss of Keller and Molly has been horrible, I know. They knew the risks, but... it's horrible. What do you think we should do?"

"I suppose all we can do is wait," Yeva said, shrugging her shoulders. "The good news is we've completed many of the main mission goals already. The final planned task for us was to start the terraforming experiment with the greenhouse devices. We're supposed to do that right before leaving, but given the current circumstances, we may need to accelerate the schedule."

Adam stretched his arms up above his head to think. "Well, let's wait it out and see if we can re-establish contact. We still have several days of food and water here in the Big Turtle. Then, maybe we'll launch the greenhouse devices. Let's take this one hour at a time."

The greenhouse devices were bombs. They were the culmination of decades worth of research — terraforming experiments planned for Mars. They were quite simple. At their core, they were small helicopter drones that carried tiny Plutonium-based atomic bombs. They differed from traditional nukes in that the warhead was designed to use up all of the Plutonium and its byproducts during the detonation. It would explode like a massive atomic bomb, but with a minimum amount of radioactive fallout.

The explosions would send debris, organic matter (hopefully), water, and dust into the atmosphere, causing an accelerated greenhouse effect. With enough of these devices, they would eventually recreate a habitable atmosphere like that of Earth. It would be complete with rain and a relatively constant temperature, albeit still cold. However, predictions estimated the full effect to take many months, if not years or decades, to stabilize. This was all in theory of course.

Everything works in theory.

Adam spent the next two days trying to establish contact with NASA, but to no avail. For a brief moment toward the end of the second day, he heard breaks in the static followed by some unintelligible yelling, but that quickly stopped. That was the last signal he ever received.

Just after breakfast the following morning, Adam and Yeva decided it was time to execute the greenhouse device experiment.

They put on their pressure suits and wandered out through the airlock. In the utility storage space on the side of Big Turtle, they found a dozen of the surprisingly small greenhouse devices. Each one was about the size of a shoebox and weighed about ten pounds on Earth — just under four pounds on Mars.

The two astronauts carried them to a designated launch spot approximately 100 feet away from Big Turtle. This distance would minimize the effect of the wind eddies swirling from the edges of the spacecraft. After setting each one down, they switched on the power button and stood back.

The top split open like a clamshell and a block sprang up about six inches. Beneath it was a round metal shaft. From that block, another block sprang up another six inches. Both of these resulting blocks unfolded into their own massive 10 foot wide rotor blades. Having these stacked counter-rotating blades eliminated any need for a complicated tail rotor system; the kind found on traditional helicopters. In the very thin Mars atmosphere, large rotor blades were necessary and they had to spin at incredibly high speeds to generate enough lift to fly.

Adam looked out upon the flock of Plutonium-carrying drone helicopters. Several of the rotors were already slowly spinning thanks to the natural winds on Mars.

"Behold, my flock of drones!" Adam yelled, laughing. "Go forth and detonate your explosive little hearts."

With the drone units now unpacked and powered up,

the two astronauts walked back into the Big Turtle through the airlock. Yeva sat down in front of the drone flight-control computer. It was specifically designed to handle a swarm of drone aircraft. It kept track of their positions and prevented them from smashing into each other. According to the user manual, this procedure was called *deconfliction*. The danger of that happening would be gone once they launched. At that point, the computer would tell each aircraft where to go and when to detonate.

Yeva set about engaging the system. Each launch was a performance. The counter-rotating blades were terrifying to watch as they spun up to speed. They looked like the world's most dangerous lawnmowers — on a planet with nearly 56 million square miles of land, but not a single blade of grass.

The rotor blades pushed enough air down to swirl up large dust clouds. Dust devils formed all around the launch area. One by one, the drones lifted up and flew away, disappearing over the horizon. Only one detonated within visual sight, but even then it must've been a hundred miles away. The red mushroom clouds rose up and began wafting through the atmosphere. It was reminiscent of the towering smoke trails that rise up from forest fires.

The whole launch process took several hours, but it would take half the day for the final detonation to occur. When the completion signal finally came, Yeva breathed a sigh of relief. She looked over at Adam with a tired frown.

"Well, that marks the official end of our main tasks here."

Adam spent the rest of the day sending out messages to NASA with the hopes of getting a reply. Nothing ever came.

The joy of today's successful drone activity was

dampened by the sense of helplessness regarding the lack of communication with Mission Control. As night fell across the ship, they each lay down in their bunks and went to sleep with the hope that communication would be established soon.

CHAPTER 26

Adam woke up to the sound of raindrops hitting the windows on the Big Turtle. In that familiar just-waking-up haze, he thought he was hearing the beginnings of a classic Texas storm, one that starts out with a few fat raindrops slapping the windows, then turning into a roar. This time, the roar never came. Just slow occasional splats on the windows. His eyelids opened completely and reality sank in.

Still on Mars, he thought disappointedly.

The weather patterns were changing faster than even the best-case scenarios had predicted. The expectation was for the process to take months, if not years. The greenhouse bombs blasted soil, soot, and dust into the swirling upper atmosphere.

After just two days, dark reddish clouds began circling the planet, causing the Mount Sharp region to experience both overcast and sunny periods. Moisture from the polar ice caps had also been blasted sky high, but it took several more days for the moist air to work its way down to the main jetstreams. After a few days of watching the dark red clouds float by, the astronauts saw white clouds appearing and disappearing until only white clouds with reddish tints were left. And after all that time, they still could not establish communications with NASA.

Yeva sat at the table, staring out the window at the rain. She heard Adam waking up and looked over at him.

"You know," she pondered, "this is probably the first rain on Mars in two thousand centuries."

"Interesting," Adam remarked. He got out of bed and walked over to the communication station, picked up the microphone, and powered it on.

"Hello Mission Control, this is Big Turtle transmitting from Mars. As I've been saying for many days now, we've completed the terraforming experiment and this morning it's actually raining. Can you believe that? If you receive this signal, please let us know. Um..., yadda, yadda, yadda," he said pathetically before turning off the equipment.

Adam walked over to the main table and sat in the chair across from Yeva. She continued staring at the drizzly rainfall outside. The pitter patter of rain sounds echoed off the windows. Adam rubbed his neck to get rid of the morning stiffness.

"A million rubles for your thoughts," Yeva coaxed.

"A million, huh? I'd settle for a ten second phone call to my family. What's there to say?" he asked hopelessly. "It's been silent too long. Our radios are working fine. I just don't get it. What do you think we should do?"

Yeva tapped her fingers on the table. She nodded her

head to imply understanding.

"We have two options as I see it. We can bide our time here and wait until Mission Control contacts us. Or, we can pack up and return home."

Adam had mixed feelings. He desperately wanted to see his wife and family, but there was unlikely to be a warm welcome when he returned. Everything he had planned for after the post-Mars mission was falling apart, the level of which depended on how much of the helmet video Mission Control received. He had to assume they'd received *enough*.

It was just self-defense, he told himself. That didn't really matter, though. He killed a charismatic astronaut and businessman loved by all Americans.

Yeva pulled him out of his daydream. She looked him in the eyes. "With Molly and Keller gone, we do have some extra water and food rations, but there is really no reason to delay the return. We've already initiated the terraforming experiment. We have rock samples. We have core samples — enough to keep the scientists busy for years. We *will* have to leave eventually. It is a mathematical certainty. Why wait?"

Adam nodded and looked up from the table.

"I think something terrible has happened back home," he said without sugarcoating his fear. "If this is just an antenna problem on the space station, they've had plenty of time to redirect all of the other deep-space transmitters toward Mars to get a message to us. *Anything*. Right now, we're just... castaways."

Yeva pounded her fist on the table, "Then we should go now! We should start the return procedures now!"

"Well, what if we're returning to a smoking rock?" he erupted. "Huh? What if something so terrible has happened that we won't survive *after* the landing?"

"Yes, that is a remote possibility," Yeva replied loudly, "but we cannot stay here forever. I think we should go immediately. Remember — the sooner we leave, the sooner you see your family."

Adam knew she was right. He told her so with a sigh. His eyes showed true worry. *What if something terrible had happened on Earth? Had he failed at the core responsibility of being a parent — to protect his family?*

Adam stared blankly at the edge of the stainless steel table. "You know, I admit, I came here for the adventure and glory, but I would trade it all for just a few more minutes with my kids."

"Well, you can talk about it *with them* when we get back," Yeva blurted with an irritated tone. "Let us initiate the return trip."

"Okay, but I have to make one more trip outside to take care of some tasks," Adam explained.

The rain stopped and the Sun shone down on their little part of Mars. The combination of heat energy and still-low atmospheric pressure made most of the moisture evaporate quickly.

Adam suited up and exited Big Turtle through the airlock, carrying the external pre-return checklist book with him. He walked around to the back of the Little Turtle and saw the dirt-covered, bedraggled parachutes lying on the ground. These chutes were supposed to be used during the final descent into the Pacific Ocean. Instead, they had saved their lives during the landing on Mars.

Adam shook the dirt from them and tried his best to

fold them back up. He carefully wrapped them with the hundred feet of deployed cable that connected them to the Little Turtle.

He climbed on top of the structure to put the three parachutes back into their hatches. After stuffing each chute into the respective hole, he delicately closed each hatch door. This was a tricky maneuver because the entire top surface of the Little Turtle was covered in fragile solar panels. For the final hatch door, he had to hang on to the long-range antenna tower sticking up from the roof. That was the only way to get leverage to close the door.

Adam purposely saved this task for the absolute last day on Mars. The parachutes were crucial to surviving the Earth reentry process. He didn't want to find out on *day one* of their arrival here that the parachutes were ruined and they were doomed. That would've destroyed morale for the team even before the Mars exploration began.

With one hand still on the antenna, Adam paused and took a look at the horizon. He couldn't believe the drastic changes that had happened since they'd arrived. Some large fluffy clouds floated over the still rust-colored landscape.

From his vantage point on the roof, he saw the two lonely graves. He stared without realizing how long. The shadow of a cloud engulfed the ship. Adam looked away from the graves and climbed down to the ground. He walked up the ramp and stepped into the airlock.

Once inside, he opened the new checklist that would prepare the facility for the return launch. Step one was to tell Mission Control that you were starting the procedure. He picked up the microphone and pushed the transmit button.

"Mission Control, this is Big Turtle. We are transmitting

in the blind here. *Again.* We hope that somebody there is getting this. The remaining crew consists of Yeva Turoskova and myself, Adam Alston. We are initiating the return phase of the mission. Estimated time of liftoff is about two hours from now. We should be home in about a month. Um, that's it. Signing off. Godspeed to us."

For the next two hours the astronauts went through more checklists. Space flight is all about checklists. The green ones, the yellow ones, and finally the red ones that involve matters of life and death.

The only part of the facility that was returning home was the part that brought them to Mars: *Little Turtle*. Adam transferred the remaining food from the living module to Little Turtle. Yeva transferred the remaining water containers. They walked back and forth like worker ants. The Little Turtle contained enough water to maintain four astronauts on the month-long return trip. However, it was better to have too much and not need it.

By early afternoon, the final walkthrough of the Big Turtle was complete. They each signed the dinner table with a Sharpie — astronaut graffiti of sorts. It read, *Yeva, Adam, and in memoriam: Molly and Keller*.

Adam looked around and let out a final sigh.

"I didn't like it here, but I'm going miss this place for some reason. We're leaving a lot of hope behind."

Yeva put her hand on his shoulder. "It feels like we have lived a lifetime here already. And not in a good way. Let us go home."

The two astronauts walked down the hallway connector to the Little Turtle and closed the door behind them. Adam opened a wall plate cover and pushed a recessed switch. The hallway connector popped off the Little Turtle, effectively disconnecting the umbilical between the two ships.

Big Turtle would sit on the surface of Mars for many years before the blowing wind and, hopefully, water-based erosion would tear it down. The onboard systems would function for another few months before the solar panels could no longer supplement the battery storage and fuel cells.

Little Turtle was once again a standalone spaceship. The two astronauts put on their space suits and helmets and clambered into their launch seats; this left them lying on their backs facing upward. Just one last checklist for fuel monitoring remained. They would only have about one minute of fuel for the conventional rocket engines to get them off the planet and into orbit. After some time circling Mars, the autopilot would take over, firing the rocket engine for a few seconds to break them out of Mars orbit. At that point the computer would fire the Murch Motor MM10 engines and the Little Turtle would slingshot away from Mars onto the long path back to Earth. The engines would stay on for most of the trip, pushing them home.

Adam turned to look at Yeva.

"Are you ready?"

She grinned a hopeful smile.

"Yes, let us go home."

Adam flipped up the red switch protector on the rocket ignition toggle. He looked at the digital countdown clock. After several minutes, it finally reached the end.

"Starting countdown: five, four, three, two, one... ignition."

He pushed the toggle switch forward. The ship shook violently as the traditional rocket engines ignited, blasting holes in the Martian soil underneath. This caused a dust storm to swirl out from under the Little Turtle. The old connector hallway crumpled up and slammed into the side of the idled Big Turtle. The cross made of American and Russian flags blew down next to the two graves.

The ship began rising skyward as expected. After just a few seconds of flight, it halted and lurched violently to one side. During today's checklist, they had forgotten to release the grounding cable. The Little Turtle was *still attached to Mars*. Adam had missed that crucial step.

"Yeva! Did you release the grounding cable?"

"No! I thought *you* did it when you repacked the parachutes!"

It was supposed to be the last item on the checklist Adam had taken outside, but he didn't remember seeing it.

Mars would not let go.

The roar got louder.

"We can't turn off these engines!" Adam screamed over the noise. "We're in serious trouble!"

He knew they only had 45 seconds of fuel left for this phase of the escape. After that, they would die on Mars along with their crewmates. His mind went into overdrive. He rapidly thought through every scenario. With Little Turtle pulling tightly on the cable, there was no way the secondary release method would work now.

Adam unlatched his seatbelt and jumped over to the console, grabbing the remote control for the mini-rover.

The ship lurched and threw Adam to the floor. He clawed back up to the window.

As the ship tugged against the grounding cable, Adam had a hard time keeping his bearings. One hand held him to the ship, and his other hand held the remote control transmitter.

He gave the remote control full throttle. Off in the distance he saw a puff of dust rise up. The little rover was racing toward them, hopping over the random soil drifts and fighting the blast from the rockets.

With his thumb on the throttle, he tried desperately to maneuver the steering stick with his other fingers. The rover came closer and closer. He steered it right toward the bottom of the ship.

"Come on baby, you gotta help us!" Adam yelled at the racing rover. "Hit that cable!"

It disappeared from view underneath the ship. A loud metallic sheering sound roared up through the floor structure.

The rover broke the grounding cable and the Little Turtle lurched violently upward. The sudden jolt caused the long-range antenna on the roof to break and fall over. It slid down the solar cell roof, ripping several panels away and falling past the window.

Adam collapsed to the floor under the intense and sudden acceleration. He tried to crawl to his seat, but the g-forces were just too much; he was pinned down.

Yeva reached over and grabbed his hand. He squeezed tight as the ship continued its ascent out of the Martian atmosphere. His other arm wrapped around the frame of his seat.

The surface escape rockets were pushing hard, but the ship hadn't left the Martian atmosphere yet. With the antenna and a few solar panels gone, the asymmetric aerodynamics caused a lot of turbulence. A low-frequency shaking grew as the ship went faster. Alarm after alarm turned on. Dozens of colorful lights were flashing. The shaking resonated with the escape-hatch door.

Boom. Boom. Boom.

Yeva focused intently on the door.

"Hang in there, hang in there," she repeated to herself.

Boom. Boom. Boom.

The door began to buckle.

A crease appeared.

Boom. Boom. Boom.

Adam looked over at the black anti-gravity cube. It broke loose from the straps he tied it down with. The cube appeared to have no idea about the intense acceleration they were experiencing. It bounced haphazardly around the cabin with so much mass that it left small dents wherever it hit. It made a clink sound as it bounced against a window. A crack in the glass began to spider, shooting out tiny chips.

Yeva stared at the pulsing door.

Boom. Boom. Boom.

One of the two hinge pins shot out of the crumpling escape-hatch door and fired across the cabin.

The anti-gravity cube slammed into the little striped cabinet where the Red Hope capsules were kept. The little cabinet door flung open and poisonous red liquid sprayed out, filling the compartment with deadly red fog.

Boom. Boom. Boom.

Screeeeeech!

The escape-hatch door blew off and spun out into the blackness of space. The cabin depressurized violently, sucking the poisonous fog out with it. The rush of air outward was so powerful that several of the interior wall panels ripped loose from their moorings and bent toward the escape-hatch hole.

Some of the water bags exploded, creating a shower of ice particles resembling frozen rain drops. The crystals fell to the floor immediately as the ship accelerated under rocket power. Yeva was ripped from her seatbelt and slammed into the console located between her and the empty hatch opening. Adam held her hand tightly to keep her from getting sucked out through the escape-hatch.

Suddenly, there was silence.

The rockets stopped; the ship was in orbit. Everything that had been pinned to the floor was suddenly floating, weightless, around the cabin interior. Hundreds of loose checklist pages floated haphazardly around Adam and Yeva, brushing against their visors. If the flight control computer was still functional, the main engine would burn for a few seconds to break the Mars orbit and then the MM10 engines would kick in and start pushing them toward Earth.

Adam would not let go of Yeva's hand. The communication headsets weren't working. He pulled her toward him and swiped the floating papers out of the way so he could see her face. She had blood pooling around her nose, but there was nothing she could do about it with her helmet on.

Adam glanced over at the small cabinet housing the poisonous Red Hope containers; there were still two left.

How ironic, he thought. Just when they could've used it, they were in the one situation where they couldn't.

Pages from the manuals and ice crystals floated

effortlessly out the open door. The sunrise peeked over the horizon, illuminating the ship exterior like a flare. A bright beam of sunlight barged in through the missing doorway. It tried to reach the two astronauts, but there was too much floating clutter protecting them. The dancing papers and ice crystals created a swarm of shadows and sparkles. Adam squinted as the bright light finally pierced his visor. He looked at Yeva again, but all he could see was the reflection of his own panicked face in her visor. His eyes darted around, thinking, searching, hoping, *accepting*.

CHAPTER 27

Earth

Fog rolled silently across a rural Texas road, billowing down a shallow hillside. As the Sun rose, the fog lifted, revealing a park meadow rarely visited anymore.

"It's all you now, Kiddo! Push the pedals!" Connie yelled as she let go of her son's bicycle.

Young Cody pedaled hard. The bike rattled loudly every time the wheels jolted over a dirt clod.

Connie could now run easily next to his bike, just like Adam used to. Cody coasted for a few feet, his wheels slowing down. The front wheel wobbled left and right before the boy and his bike fell over together. Connie knelt down next to him.

"You did so great, Honey. I bet you go even farther next time. I'll be right next to you. I won't let you get hurt."

Cody looked up at his Mom and grinned with a smile, happily displaying the two new front teeth that had finally grown in.

"I know, Mom. Let me try again."

A large black sedan turned off the main road and lumbered into the parking lot. It crunched over the gravel and pulled up next to Connie's minivan. She looked up toward it. A slow smile swept over her face as she walked back toward the parking lot. Cody wheeled his bike behind her. A familiar man exited the car and started walking toward them.

"Hi, Connie! Hi, Cody!" the friendly man bellowed.

"Long time, no see, Chris. Cody, you remember Mr. Tankovitch, right?" Connie asked.

Chris leaned down and shook Cody's hand.

"Young man, I bet you're a bicycle expert by now. NASA may need you in the astronaut program when you grow up."

The little boy smiled politely as he shook his head side to side. He wanted nothing to do with space travel.

"Mommy, can I go play with my Rescue Bots?"

She leaned down to speak with Cody at eye level.

"Sure. Go ahead, and put your seat belt on, too."

She patted him on the head as he put the bike in the back of the minivan. Cody climbed in over the bike and crawled through the interior, finally flopping down into the back booster seat.

Connie crossed her arms and let out a comfortable sigh.

"So what brings you all the way out here today?"

Chris smiled. "A lot has happened since we lost contact with them a few months ago."

"That's quite the understatement," Connie replied.

Chris looked down at the field and then back at Connie.

"From the way you were running with Cody, can I assume the experimental back surgery worked?" Chris asked.

"It's been like a miracle cure. I'm all healed."

Connie did a slow pirouette on the gravel to demonstrate how her spine operation had succeeded.

Chris laughed. "That's fantastic, Connie. I'm glad it worked out so well. I know Adam really wanted that for you."

An uncomfortable silence rose up between them.

"Chris, I'm sorry that you lost your job at NASA. I know it meant the world to you."

Chris chuckled.

"That's just the way it works when you're in a job appointed by the president. Besides, there's a lot of people in the world right now, especially Houston and Moscow, that have it harder than me. I made out pretty easy, if I may say so."

"You know, Chris, I wonder if the Russians are recovering as quickly as we are. It was a terrible thing; *all those lives...*"

"We lost a lot of good people," Chris admitted. "So did they. Both countries are rebuilding, but it's a slow process. We will overcome this."

Chris moved some gravel around with his foot to avoid what he had to say next.

"A friend of mine who still works at NASA told me about some, um, *new* information. I wanted to share it with you before the news media gets it. This is strictly confidential, okay? It's serious stuff."

"Yes, of course," she answered in a worried tone.

"Okay. Some of the surviving engineers at NASA finally

got the deep-space antennas at Goldstone back online last month. That's a remote antenna complex out west. They were able to re-establish partial communication with the Curiosity Rover, but without the long-range antenna on the space station, there was no way to communicate with the Little Turtle. NASA was in the process of building a duplicate of the long-range antenna here on Earth when, suddenly, the new Mission Control Center up in Fort Worth reported getting a beacon signal from the Little Turtle."

Connie looked confused.

"I don't know what a beacon signal is. Does that mean that the ship started working again? Is the signal coming all the way from Mars?"

Her expression turned to one of hopefulness.

"Not exactly," Chris admitted. "The beacon signal is a simple data stream that the autopilot sends out as it gets *near* Earth. It uses a short-range transmitter on the Little Turtle. The main purpose of the beacon signal is to help Mission Control lock onto its position. It's a bit of a last minute duct-tape fix for a design problem we thought might pop up."

Chris looked over at the minivan and then back at Connie. He continued, "The Little Turtle is notoriously hard to track with radar. It's because the faceted outside is, by unfortunate design, very *stealthy* and hard to track. Normally, the long range antenna makes it light up like a Christmas tree on radar. Not this time though. The beacon signal caught them by surprise."

"Okay, but what does it mean?" Connie asked.

Chris looked over the top of his glasses at Connie.

"It means the *ship* is still alive. The crew was able to at least launch off the surface of Mars. It means the Little Turtle is coming home."

Connie's eyes welled up with tears. "You mean, somebody on board is still steering it? Maybe? Possibly?"

Chris shook his head.

"No. Well, there's a remote chance...," Chris trailed off.

He looked down to search for the right words.

"There's really no chance they're still alive. It's most likely been on autopilot for the last few months. I doubt the crew could've lived this long with the three of them on board. Besides, the beacon signal says that only one emergency life support system was activated after takeoff. Whatever happened wasn't good. I wanted to tell you firsthand before this hit the news. I don't want to give you any ideas that Adam is coming home alive. It's just not in the cards."

Connie rocked side to side, crying.

"But there is a *chance*? Some hope?" she asked through all the tears.

Chris shook his head again.

"I'm so sorry, Connie. I don't think so."

She brought her hand up to wipe away the tears that crowded on her cheeks and looked away from Chris, unable to make eye contact.

"Okay, I gotcha. I understand," Connie whimpered.

She looked up at Chris suddenly.

"Do you think he died a *foolish* death?"

Chris didn't expect a question like that.

"I'm..." he said before pausing again for several seconds. Connie could tell that he desperately wanted to tell her something.

"Let me answer you this way. I'm not supposed to tell

anybody this yet — I'm not even supposed to know about this — but we finally figured out what the early Martian creation was that ultimately brought down their society. The translation was very difficult because it used chemical equations that our chemists didn't understand until just recently."

Chris paused. His mind searched for the right words.

"You might think that an advanced culture like theirs would've touted interplanetary space-travel or anti-gravity as their quintessential achievement, but most of the walls in that room were a presentation of a chemical equation and how to manufacture it. Our own chemists are trying to synthesize it here on Earth right now. The Martians invented a way, a medicine of some type, to control cell growth rates. They could slow it down, speed it up, or maybe even stop it."

Connie furled her eyebrows in confusion.

"I don't get why that's important, Chris," Connie said, wiping a hair from her face.

"Being able to control cell growth rates has *far reaching* consequences. In addition to slowing down the aging process, they effectively cured cancer and any other disease that has to do with runaway cell growth. To them, treating cancer was probably like we treat heartburn today. Take some medicine, and the cancer goes away. They didn't have to worry about exposure to carcinogens because, well, anybody who got cancer could be cured. They were smart enough to know that their greatest achievement was something that would save the lives of so many people. Not interplanetary flight. Not anti-gravity. Just a cure for something that has dogged us since the dawn of time."

Chris crossed his arms and continued explaining.

"Unfortunately, their society wasn't ready for the results of their discovery. Mars is smaller, so their food resources couldn't keep up with the exploding population. They destroyed their planet by trying to keep everybody fed. Our experts are sure that Earth is different. We can absorb that kind of population growth. That's what they say anyway."

Chris rubbed his chin with his hand before continuing.

"We're not there yet, though. Part of the manufacturing process requires the use of anti-gravity and, unfortunately, that technology is either still on Mars or — if we're lucky — inside the Little Turtle, on its way home. That's the vital missing piece. With cancer rates skyrocketing from the bomb radiation fallout, I hope to God they put that cube on that spaceship."

Chris walked closer and put his hand on her shoulder.

"Connie, your family's sacrifice will ultimately save the human race from infinite misery. Rest assured: Adam did *many* great things."

Connie's eyes overflowed with tears.

"Yes, but I still miss him so much," she cried as she hugged Chris. "It sounds like he went there for a good reason, then?"

"Yes," Chris answered. "He went there for the *best* reasons."

Connie nodded her head and wiped her eyes.

"Okay, Chris. Well, thank you for coming all the way out here. I won't tell the kids about the news; I don't want to give them false hope. They're having a hard enough time as it is."

Connie walked to the minivan and opened the door. Her head tilted up; she looked over at Chris who hadn't moved. She climbed into her seat and sat there silently. Cody played with his robot toys in the back seat. She started the engine, pulled onto the road and drove away.

Chris stood there, reflecting on what had taken place: his journey all the way from visiting Keller Murch's beach house to getting a team of astronauts to Mars. He knew much more about what Adam had done on Mars, but he would *never* tell Connie about it.

Chris walked toward his car, but slowed down. He paused and changed direction, meandering down a dirt bike path that ran near a casting pond. There was no bench nearby, so he sat down in the inviting grass to enjoy the quiet solitude. He had a peaceful view of the calm water right in front of him.

Birds flew overhead as he watched the puffy cumulus clouds consume the bright blue sky. The strong smell of freshly cut grass wafted past. It reminded him of that night spent observing Halley's Comet with his dad. Chris looked to his left and then to his right. Finally, he looked straight upward and said, "Show me a miracle, Adam. Make me a believer again."

Somewhere just beyond the Moon, a ship raced home toward Earth, still several days out. The spacecraft closely resembled a haggard and fragile turtle shell. Contained within its delicate walls was a small cube-shaped gift of technology from ancient ancestors of mankind — a gift to ourselves across an ocean of space and time.

The escape-hatch door was gone. In its place, the opening was now sealed over by a stack of metal cabinet doors, located on the inside and held in place with cabin air pressure alone — the handiwork of desperate souls. Only half of the MM10 motors were operating. Extended out from the ship was a long nylon strap. The far end of the strap was wrapped around the waist of a very still space suit.

The porthole windows around the ship were cracked, but still in place; all fogged except for one. Barely visible behind that window was a solitary set of green eyes, staring outward through the glass. Bloodshot and barely blinking, they were transfixed on the familiar ocean-covered planet floating in front of them. The eyes were exhausted from the strain of not knowing the right thing to do for so long.

Now, they trembled with *blue* hope.

ABOUT THE AUTHOR

John Dreese enjoys stories about adventure, technology, business and people. Red Hope was his debut novel. The second (and last) book in the Red Hope series is now available. It is called BLUE HOPE.

If you have any comments or questions, please feel free to send an email:

JJDreese@yahoo.com

Twitter:

http://www.twitter.com/JJDreese/

Facebook:

http://www.facebook.com/JohnDreeseAuthor/

BOOKS BY JOHN DREESE

Red Hope

Blue Hope
(Book 2 of the Red Hope Series)